SEX FO

——Top model

Police yesterday raided the Barrington Club, arresting the owner, Morgan Baxter, 36, on suspicion of living off immoral earnings. It is rumored that among club members were a number of VIPs, judges and politicians. No names have been released by police, except for that of Baxter's girlfriend——model Alex Sherwood——arrested alongside him.

Miss Sherwood, an attractive blonde, 24, looked drawn and pensive as she was released after a night in the cells. She denied any involvement in the club or knowledge of Baxter's activities and stressed that her relationship with Baxter was one of platonic friendship. It is believed that Sherwood immediately left the country.

KAY THORPE was born in Sheffield, England, in 1935. She tried out a variety of jobs after leaving school. Writing began as a hobby, becoming a way of life only after she had her first completed novel accepted for publication in 1968. Since then she's written over fifty novels, and lives now with her husband, son, German shepherd dog and lucky black cat on the outskirts of Chesterfield in Derbyshire. Her interests include reading, hiking and travel.

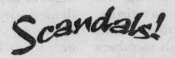

Have you heard the latest?

Get ready for the next outrageous Scandal

RED-HOT AND RECKLESS

by

Miranda Lee (#1930)

All will be revealed in January 1998!

KAY
THORPE

The Rancher's Mistress

Harlequin Books

TORONTO • NEW YORK • LONDON
AMSTERDAM • PARIS • SYDNEY • HAMBURG
STOCKHOLM • ATHENS • TOKYO • MILAN
MADRID • WARSAW • BUDAPEST • AUCKLAND

ISBN 0-373-11924-0

THE RANCHER'S MISTRESS

First North American Publication 1997.

Copyright © 1997 by Kay Thorpe.

CHAPTER ONE

TAKING in the panoramic view of rolling grasslands and timbered mountain slopes, Alex felt well and truly over the rainbow. Wyoming! The name itself conjured up images of hard-thewed cowboys astride spirited steeds, of thundering herds of cattle and whistling lariats. That the old Western films she had loved as a teenager would bear little resemblance to today's reality she didn't need telling, but it did no harm to dream.

'How long will it take us to reach the Lazy Y?' she asked the man at the wheel of the station wagon, savouring the name.

'An hour or so,' he said. 'We'll be in good time for supper. Hope you're not on a diet. The food is really something. Needs to be too, considering what it costs to spend a week on the ranch. Taking in dudes is a pretty lucrative business.'

'It's a working ranch too, though, isn't it? At least, that's the impression you gave in your letter.'

'It's that all right. Cal would sooner give up breathing than cattle-breeding.'

Catching the acerbic note, Alex shot her brother a glance. Handsome as he'd been at eighteen, when she'd last seen him in the flesh, he was even more so at twenty-six: blond hair bleached by the sun, features hardened into manhood. They had often been taken for twins when they were children, despite the two years between them. The resemblance was still there, of course, though obviously nowhere near as pronounced.

5

Whether the empathy they had shared could be re-established after eight years apart was something else.

'Do you get on all right with him?' she queried.

The shrug was noncommittal. 'Well enough.'

Not exactly 'buddy-buddy', Alex gathered—which wasn't all that surprising, she supposed, considering the circumstances.

'How about the guests?' she said. 'Do they join in with the general ranch work too?'

'The ones who want to. Amazing how many seem to look on working their butts off fencing and riding herd as part and parcel of what they're paying for!'

'Perhaps they're living out a private fantasy,' Alex suggested lightly. 'I always wanted to be a cowgirl myself.'

Greg's quick grin momentarily restored the boyish look she remembered. 'I'd say modelling was the better choice.'

She gave a wry smile. 'Not so much a choice as an enticement. If I hadn't been spotted by that photographer, I'd never have thought of it as a career. The problem now is having no particular qualifications to fall back on. Something you tend not to take too much into account at seventeen.'

'You're hardly over the hill yet,' Greg observed, slanting a swift, appraising glance at the tumble of honey-blonde hair and finely sculpted profile.

'Where photographic work is concerned, I'm fast getting that way.' Alex took care to keep her tone matter-of-fact. 'I've had a good run, but it's time I started thinking about doing something else with my life.'

'You know best, I suppose.' He paused briefly. 'Anything in particular in mind?'

'I've done promotional work from time to time. A

company I worked for last year offered me a permanent job selling costume jewellery in stores.'

Greg pulled a face. 'Sounds a bit dull after the kind of life you must have led to date.'

'I haven't done that much candle-burning,' Alex replied drily. 'Riotous late nights aren't to be recommended for anyone due to face a camera next day.'

'You could always find yourself a rich husband. With your looks it should be a doddle!'

'If I marry anyone at all,' she declared on an emphatic note, 'it certainly won't be for money!'

'You always were a romantic,' he scoffed.

She might have been once, Alex reflected. If the last few years hadn't rid her of her illusions, the last few weeks certainly had!

'Was it love at first sight for you and Margot?' she asked, putting the memories resolutely aside. 'You said you met in Las Vegas.'

'That's right. Some friends she was visiting brought her to the nightclub where I was working behind the bar. We were married a week later.'

'And you call *me* the romantic!'

The vivid blue eyes, so like her own, fixed on the near-empty road ahead, he said smoothly, 'She wanted everything done and dusted before Cal could put his spoke in.'

'He's her brother, not her guardian. Surely—'

'You wouldn't know it at times. He treats her more like sixteen than twenty!'

Perhaps with some reason, Alex thought, trying to be fair-minded about it. Leaping into marriage with a virtual stranger was hardly sensible behaviour at any age. Greg hadn't answered the first half of the question, which might suggest that love hadn't been *his* prime motive. After drifting about the world for so long, a set-up like the Lazy Y had to have some pulling power.

Scant evidence on which to make that kind of deduction, she chided herself. The man seated beside her was different in many ways from the boy she had grown up with, but that didn't mean he'd become an out-and-out opportunist. She, of all people, should know better than to take anyone or anything at face value.

Twelve when their father had died, Alex had accepted her mother's remarriage less than a year later rather more easily than Greg, who had bitterly resented the intrusion. His departure after four years of unceasing animosity to join a group intending to work their way round the world had come almost as a relief at first, but she had missed him badly as the days stretched into weeks and months. Letters had been few and far between, the content woefully inadequate. The group he was travelling with had gradually dwindled until there were only three of them left, but he'd never shown any sign of wanting to come home.

The news just a couple of weeks ago of his marriage and move to Wyoming had been a double shock as she had believed him to be still somewhere in Australia. Coming at a time when she so badly needed to get away from it all, his suggestion that she take a trip over to meet her new in-laws had seemed like manna from heaven. By the time she got back, the whole sorry business would hopefully be old news.

'Mum sends her love,' she said now, adding tentatively, 'She hopes you'll see your way to visiting some time.'

'Not while *he's* still around,' was the more than half-anticipated answer.

'It's been eight years,' Alex protested. 'You might find him easier to get along with now.'

'And cows might fly!' Greg shook his head. 'No way am I going back there. Mum made her choice when she married him.'

Alex gave up, recognising finality when she heard it. She could be obdurate herself when it came to something she felt strongly about, but this went beyond that.

'Was it your brother-in-law's suggestion that you invite me out to stay?' she asked, by way of changing the subject.

'More Margot's. She's looking forward to meeting you. She wanted to come with me to the airport, but I thought we should have some time on our own to start with. We've a lot of catching up to do.' He put his foot down to overtake the only other vehicle in sight, shooting the speedometer needle over the seventy mark in total disregard of the speed limits and earning himself a horn blast from a gesticulating driver. 'You never mentioned your own love life in your letters,' he added, undisturbed by the censure. 'Always providing I got them all, that is.'

'I'd doubt it. You were hardly ever in one place long enough.' Alex ran her hand under the silky curtain of hair at her nape, circling her small, firm chin in an effort to ease aching muscles. 'I hope there's plenty of hot water on tap. I feel in dire need of a shower!'

'There's plenty of everything on tap,' Greg assured her. 'And you didn't answer the question.'

'I didn't realise you were asking one.' She circled her chin in the other direction, concentrating on the movement. 'If I haven't mentioned men, it's probably because there's been no one special enough to write about.'

'Maybe you'll meet your one and only out here, then.'

Her laugh was short. 'I'll hardly be here long enough to develop any meaningful relationships.'

'You never know. One look might be all it takes. You said you always wanted to be a cowgirl. This could be your chance.'

'It could at that.' Alex summoned a suitably flippant note. 'I'll keep my eyes skimmed for a likely prospect.'

'Don't bother with the herd, go for the head bull,' he advised. 'Cal's thirty-four. It's high time he got hitched.'

'Perhaps he's married to his work. And I didn't realise he was so much older than Margot,' she tagged on contemplatively.

'Her mother was into her forties when she had her. She died giving birth. Cal took over when his father was killed ten years ago. He started taking in dudes when beef prices went way down a couple of years later. There's no call for any supplementary income these days but he still keeps them coming. Full capacity most summer weeks.'

'It's obviously a popular way to spend a vacation.' Alex could think of no better way herself. 'Are there likely to be any horses going spare? It's been ages since I had chance of a ride.'

'You'll be able to take your pick,' Greg confirmed. 'Plenty of other activities too. Ever been hot-air ballooning?'

'No—though I wouldn't mind trying it. Not that I'm expecting to be treated like a paying guest. There must be plenty I can do to help out while I'm here.'

The thought alone was pleasurable. Stretching long, trouser-clad legs, Alex leaned back in her seat, determined to make the most of this opportunity. Mending fences, riding herd—it all sounded like heaven! Dorothy could have her Oz. She was going to be living her own fantasy this next week or two!

She must have dozed off after that. When she opened her eyes again the mountains were almost on top of them. They had left the main road, she saw, sitting up. The one they were on now was narrow, the surface roughened, the edges fenced off from the grassland either side. Horses grazed the immediate left-hand pasture.

'Sorry about that,' she said, stifling a yawn. 'Flying always tires me out. How much further?'

'We've been on Lazy Y for the last ten minutes,' Greg returned. 'That's the homestead up ahead.'

Nestling at the head of the broad valley, the cluster of buildings resolved themselves into one large, central structure flanked by barns, with more buildings scattered among the trees beyond. Corrals occupied the foreground, one of them containing a mixed group of people in the process of unsaddling their mounts after a ride. Voices and laughter carried across on the still evening air as Greg brought the station wagon to a halt in front of the main house and killed the engine.

'Back at the ranch,' he said on an ironical note. 'Cal's probably still out there somewhere, but Margot will be around.'

Alex got out of the vehicle, easing her limbs and breathing in the sparkling air with enjoyment. No matter how warm the days, at six-thousand feet Wyoming summer evenings were cool; she could already feel the drop in temperature through the thin cotton of her shirt.

Her jacket was in the car where she had tossed it. She leaned in to get it, body supple as a willow, though a great deal more shapely, straightening again to view the house as she slid her arms into the sleeves. Two storeys of mellowed timber fronted by wide verandas, it fulfilled her mental image of what a ranch-house should look like to a degree. There was even an iron triangle hanging from a beam, complete with dangling metal rod. Used to summon guests over to the house for meals, she hoped. That would really add to the atmosphere!

The girl who appeared on the veranda was no detriment to the picture either. Small and slender in her jeans and blue and white checked shirt, and sporting a riotous crop of chestnut curls above a piquantly pretty face, she came running eagerly down the three broad steps.

'Hi, Alex! It's great to meet you at last!' She went up on her toes to deliver a kiss on the cheek, laughing unaffectedly when her aim went a bit askew. 'Aren't you lovely and tall! Should have known you would be! Greg told me how much alike the two of you were.' She stood back to direct a frank appraisal. 'You're more gorgeous even than I imagined! Is your hair natural?'

'I've been known to have it streaked a time or two, but, otherwise, yes,' Alex confirmed, laughing with her. 'And you're pretty gorgeous yourself, sister-in-law.'

'Oh, gosh, we are, aren't we? Sisters-in-law, I mean. I always wanted a sister!'

'So how about saying thank you to the man who provided you with one?' said Greg.

Margot flung her arms about his neck, the sheer adoration in her sparkling hazel eyes catching at Alex's heartstrings. 'Thank you, honey! Thank you, thank you, thank you!'

'No need to overdo it,' he admonished. He kissed the end of her nose and put her back on her feet, turning her about to deliver a light slap on her pert behind. 'To duty, wench, or it's going to be supper-time before we're ready for it. Take Alex up to her room while I get the bags.'

A regular master of the house, thought Alex amusedly, moving to accompany the younger girl indoors. Not that Margot appeared to have any objections to being ordered around. That she was totally overboard where Greg was concerned was only too patently obvious.

It was too early as yet to say whether Greg returned any real depth of feeling, although, judging from his attitude just now, Alex somehow doubted it. Tolerant affection was the closest she could come to describing it, yet they'd been married little more than three months. Hardly time for the honeymoon to be over.

The house was no disappointment inside, either. Arches gave access to what looked like a vast living room on one side of the wide, pine-floored hall, and an equally vast dining room on the other, the central staircase branching left and right to open galleries.

The room Alex was to occupy was at the front of the house. Timber all the way through, it had woven rugs scattered across the floor and a hand-crocheted cover on the king-sized bed. The two windows were small and multi-paned. Designed to better resist the winter cold, Alex judged, loving the ambience of the place.

'There's a bathroom two doors down, and another the other side but no *en suite* I'm afraid,' said Margot apologetically. 'The guest cabins all have private facilities, but Cal said we'd knocked things about enough without trying to incorporate them here. Apart from the living and dining rooms, we don't have paying guests in the house anyway. I hope you'll be comfortable,' she added, looking round. 'It isn't exactly luxurious.'

'It couldn't be better,' Alex assured her. 'None of it could!'

She went over to a window, looking down on the scene below with elation bubbling inside her at the thought of the days to come. Humping saddles, the recently returned party was headed for one of the barns, leaving their mounts in the confines of the corral. Another group of riders was coming in through the over-barred gateway, with its swinging sign. A working party this time, she guessed, spying coiled lariats hanging from one or two pommels. The real McCoy!

She watched the men dismount and start unsaddling, her eyes coming to rest on one lean and rangy figure in a beige shirt. The horse he was stripping was lean and rangy too, its hindquarters packed with muscular power. A fitting partnership, she thought, studying the taut stretch of blue jeans across hard male hemispheres.

'Oh, good, the boys are back,' exclaimed Margot, coming to stand beside her. 'That's my brother in the fawn shirt. We're not a bit alike, as you can see even from here. He's a Forrester through and through, whereas I take after my mother's side. Cal more or less brought me up. I was only ten when Dad was killed. I owe him an awful lot.'

'He only did what any brother would do in the same circumstances,' said Greg, a trifle brusquely, from the doorway. 'Don't make a hero out of him.'

Margot laughed, apparently oblivious to any implied criticism. 'Cal would be the last to want that. Can I help you unpack?' she added ingenuously to Alex as the two cases were lifted onto the bed. 'I'll bet you have some lovely things!'

'Judging from the weight, there's a lot of them for certain,' commented Greg on a lighter note. 'Show me the woman who can go anywhere without taking her whole wardrobe!'

'Show me the man who can refrain from making the same old comment,' retorted Alex, equally lightly. 'I didn't bring anything particularly dressy, Margot, but I'd be grateful for some help in putting what I have brought away.'

'You've only just time for that shower before supper,' Greg warned her. 'Less than half an hour.'

A shower wasn't going to take her more than five minutes, Alex could have told him, and she certainly wasn't going to be piling on make-up for the evening, but she took the point. Apart from what she needed for now, the unpacking could wait.

'I'd better go and freshen up myself,' said Margot. 'You don't need to go to any great trouble, by the way. Nobody does.' She directed a bright-eyed smile at the other girl. 'I'm really glad to have you here, Alex. The guests are fine, but they don't stay around long enough to get to know all that well. Greg says you used to ride a lot. Do you still?'

'Not as often as I'd like to,' Alex acknowledged.

'Well, you can catch up here. We've over seventy head to choose from. I don't usually ride with the guests on short sessions, but I often go on the day-longs. They can be real fun.'

'For some,' commented Greg, bringing an apologetic expression to his wife's face.

'I know Cal's been driving you hard, honey, but it's only because he wants you to know how to run things, so that you can take over if needed.'

'Sure he does.' Greg didn't try to hide the scepticism. 'Anyway, it's time we were out of here. You can fill Alex in on the rest of it later.'

Alex stayed where she was for a moment or two after they'd gone, a line between her brows as she reflected on the latter conversation. That Greg wasn't too enthused about ranch work was apparent, yet what had he expected of life on a working ranch? It was probably true that in every relationship there was one who felt more than the other, but in his and Margot's case the balance looked to be far too one-sided.

Shelving the matter for the moment, she moved to unlock one of the cases and extract her toilet bag and a wrap. First the shower, then she could decide what to wear for the evening.

There was no one in sight when she emerged onto the gallery, although she could hear voices coming from below. The bathroom proved both spacious and well-appointed, with a separate shower-cubicle in addition to the oversized bath. There were towels over the rails and more folded on racks above the bath, thick and soft and huge. Big country, big everything! she thought humorously.

As Greg had promised, there was no shortage of hot water. Accustomed to the low pressure back in her flat, she was almost knocked off her feet by the sheer force of it. Gasping, she turned the control down a couple of notches, glad of the cap protecting her hair. There wouldn't have been time to dry it before supper and, while casual might be the order of the day, she certainly wouldn't have felt comfortable sitting down to table with her hair dripping down her back.

Lulled by the warm flow, she stood for a few moments just enjoying it before starting to wash. Normally she cream-cleansed her face, in the interests of keeping her skin moisturised for the camera, but tonight she threw caution to the winds and applied a luxurious lather instead, relishing the feel of it, the fresh smell of it in her nostrils.

The sudden stinging pain as the suds found their way beneath her eyelids was excruciating. Eyes screwed up and watering, she rinsed off hastily and thrust open the shower door to grope for the towel she had left hanging on the convenient hook, only to feel it slide from her wet fingers onto the floor.

'Let me help,' said a deep male voice on a satirical note, freezing her where she stood.

Squinting through the tears, she saw the same lean and rangy figure she had watched earlier flick another towel from the rail in passing and the next moment was enveloped in it, with one free end offered in order for her to wipe her still streaming eyes.

Mingled embarrassment and anger conquered the pain. This was hardly the way she had anticipated meeting her host for the first time. He was making no attempt to move away, studying her with eyes the colour of burnished steel, a faint twist at the corners of his strongly defined mouth. A strong face altogether: skin taut over hard male cheekbones, jawline clean and forceful, the whole surmounted by a thick sweep of dark hair. At five feet nine in her bare feet, Alex considered herself a fair height, but he topped her by a good six inches.

'Better?' he asked.

'Fine,' she returned, struggling to hang onto some thread of composure. 'Are you in the habit of just walking in on people?'

'The door wasn't locked,' he said without apology.

'You must have heard the shower running!'

'Not through the door.'

'So the least you could have done was back straight out again!'

'You looked in need of assistance,' he returned imperturbably. 'Why the concern? I wouldn't have thought you had any hang-ups about nudity in your line.'

Her first instinct was to hotly deny the implication,

her second and more compelling one to poke him in the eye, if only metaphorically. He wasn't the first to take it for granted that stripping down to the bare essentials was the only way to make a living in the modelling world, and he almost certainly wouldn't be the last, but that didn't make it any less aggravating.

'I suppose you didn't see anything you haven't seen a thousand times before at that!' she countered scathingly.

His lips widened in a brief, derisive smile. 'A thousand might be stretching it a piece. If you're through, I wouldn't mind getting in there myself.'

'By all means.' Clutching the far from secure towel to her, Alex moved to pass him as he stepped to one side, promptly tripped over a trailing edge of towel and was saved from measuring her length only by the speed of Cal Forrester's reactions. Held by the arm he had shot about her waist, with the slipping towel threatening to expose her assets to even closer scrutiny, she found dignity taking second place to the sudden vital awareness of his hard masculinity. 'The head bull', Greg had called him, but bulls were big and cumbersome, not lean and lithe. She felt her stomach muscles contract.

'Better watch your step,' he said, letting go of her. 'You seem pretty accident-prone.'

'I will, don't worry,' she retorted, pulling herself together. 'Thanks again for the…assistance. I'd have been lost without you.'

The satire engendered a sudden glint in the grey eyes. 'Any time.'

Alex made her escape without further mishap, gathering her wrap and slippers from the chair where she had left them as she went. As first impressions went she had certainly made an impact, she reflected wryly. Not that Cal Forrester had looked all that impressed, she had to admit.

Taking a look in the dressing-table mirror back in her room, she could hardly blame him. With her hair still tucked under the shower-cap and her eyes reddened by the soap, she looked far from a pretty sight. She dragged off the cap to allow her hair to tumble down about her shoulders, dropping the towel to reach for her wrap.

Slenderly curved at waist and hip, breasts high and firm, legs long and shapely, she had received many offers of nude work over the years, but it had never attracted her. She'd advertised everything from hosiery to make-up, modelled catalogue clothing and hostessed a television quiz-show for a couple of series, among other things, but had never quite managed to gain one of the real big-time contracts that would have made her a household name. Not that it mattered any more. She was through with that part of her life for good.

Throwing on a pair of harem trousers and a loose, silky top, she put a brush through her hair and applied a layer of amber lipstick. Her brows and lashes were dark enough not to need any enhancement, not that she would have bothered even if they hadn't been. She much preferred to go natural when she wasn't working.

The thought of seeing Cal Forrester again after that bathroom fiasco brought warmth to her cheeks. Right as she'd no doubt been in taking it that hers was far from the first female body he'd seen in the nude, it made little difference to her feelings when it came to her own exposure. She was no prude, but neither was she an exhibitionist—although he obviously took her for such.

What she certainly wasn't going to do was let him see any discomfiture on her part, she told herself firmly. Let him make what assumptions he liked. What could a jumped-up cowboy stuck out here in the back of beyond know about it anyway?

Coming from just below her window, the sudden and enthusiastic clanging of iron on iron made her jump. The anticipated summons to supper, she assumed. The sun was lowering fast, gilding the edges of the clouds and spreading deep shadows across the landscape. Whatever she might feel about the owner, the Lazy Y was no disappointment so far, Alex acknowledged. She couldn't wait to sample the rest.

CHAPTER TWO

STILL closed when she emerged from her room, the next door along opened, as if on cue, just as she reached it. Dressed now in pale grey trousers and black shirt open on the brown column of his throat, the Lazy Y's owner looked less of a cowboy but no less of a threat to her peace of mind as he ran his eyes over her, that same, derisive little smile plucking at his lips.

'I guess I neglected to welcome you properly back there,' he said. 'Other things on my mind.' He put out a hand, one dark brow lifting sardonically at her involuntary withdrawal. 'It's to shake, that's all.'

Biting back the caustic retort, Alex extended her own hand, tensing as the long brown fingers closed briefly about it. There was no disputing his physical charisma; he radiated vibrant masculinity from every pore. She could sense the latent power in that leanly muscled build.

'It's good of you to give me the opportunity to see Greg again,' she said, doing her best to conceal her reactions. 'I really am grateful.'

His shrug was dismissive. 'No big deal. Let's go and eat.'

Margot came out from one of the rooms opposite as they moved towards the stairs. She was still wearing jeans, though the blue and white shirt had been replaced by a plain white one. She looked at Alex with an admiration untainted by any hint of feminine jealousy.

21

'You look wonderful!' she exclaimed. 'Isn't she just *gorgeous*, Cal?'

'Without a doubt,' he agreed on a dry note. 'A regular Helen of Troy!'

Capable of launching a regular wallop if pushed much further! thought Alex darkly, fixing a smile on her face for Margot's benefit.

'I think I might be a little over-dressed,' she said.

Margot shook her head emphatically. 'Oh, no, you're just right! Everyone knows Greg's sister is a model. They'd all be disappointed if you turned up looking ordinary. Not that you could, anyway,' she added quickly. 'Look ordinary, I mean. You're not—'

'I'd quit while you're ahead,' advised her brother.

She wrinkled her nose at him. 'Alex knows what I mean.'

'All the way,' Alex assured her. 'And I'm flattered.' She fell into step with her sister-in-law to descend the stairs, leaving Cal to follow on behind. 'Greg already go down, did he?'

'No, but he won't be a minute. I'd have waited for him but, like he says, we're not joined at the hip.'

A pretty insensitive thing to say to a new bride, Alex reflected, doubting if Margot was quite as impervious as she appeared to be on the surface. Greg needed to prac- tise some tender loving care.

People were flooding into the dining room, the ma- jority of them dressed the way Margot was, with only a couple of the women wearing skirts. There was just the one long table, with no particular seat allocation from what Alex could gather.

Cal pulled out a chair for her halfway down the table and took the one next to her himself, introducing her to those within earshot. Seated down at the other end of the table, Margot looked to be deep in animated conversation with her own nearest neighbours.

'Greg tells us you're pretty big in Europe, Alex,' said one of the women.

'Greg exaggerates,' Alex replied lightly. 'I'm just one of many.'

'Modest as they come!' declared her brother, passing behind her on his way to the chair left vacant at Margot's side. 'Hi, everybody! Had a good day?'

The ensuing chorus established that everyone had indeed. Glad to be out of the limelight, Alex listened with enjoyment for the following few minutes as one after another expounded on events.

Eighteen was the lower age limit for guests, Greg had told her, though most of this group were in their thirties and forties, with one couple approaching retirement age from the look of them. Children would be too much of a responsibility on a working ranch, she guessed.

None of the men she had seen riding in with Cal were present, which meant that the hands must have their own dining quarters. Not quite the classless society she had visualised, then.

She was vitally conscious of the closeness of Cal's knee to hers beneath the chequered cloth, steeling herself not to jerk away on the couple of occasions that they momentarily touched. The degree of physical awareness he aroused in her was undeniable. Like being connected to the national grid, she thought whimsically.

Judging from the way some of the other women reacted to him, she wasn't on her own in finding him pretty electrifying either. Probably as much to do with what he did for a living as his general appearance. There was something inherently alluring about cowboys—even modern-day ones.

Greg hadn't exaggerated about the food. It left little to be desired either in quantity or quality. Alex had never seen steaks as big or in such profusion, never eaten chicken that tasted the way this did. The vegetables were home-grown, with three varieties of potato alone. She had no room left for the banana cream pie or fruit cobbler that followed.

The whole party adjourned to the veranda for coffee afterwards, leaving the two women who had served up the meal to clear away. Darkness was coming down fast, the stars already twinkling in a sky of grey velvet. The jet lag Alex had been conscious of earlier seemed to have dissipated. She felt exhilarated, eager for the morrow when she could maybe start doing some of the things she yearned to do. With staff on hand to take care of the general housework and cooking there was obviously no need of help in that direction, which left her free to apply herself in others. All she had to do was prove herself capable.

Cal was seated nearby. One leg lifted carelessly over the other knee, hands linked behind his head, he looked surprisingly relaxed. Surprising because Alex hadn't imagined him the type to spend an evening lazing around with the guests. He had hardly spoken a word to her during supper. Not that he'd had very much opportunity, she supposed, considering the way the woman who had seated herself on his other side had monopolised his attention.

She stole a glance at him, feeling a sudden frisson down her spine as the grey eyes turned unexpectedly her way.

'You must be finding this very dull compared with what you'd normally be doing of an evening,' he commented.

'Not in the least,' she denied. 'I like to get up early, so I'm very rarely late out of bed.'

There was mockery in the slant of his mouth. 'Always alone?'

Alex looked back at him steadily. 'I don't really think that concerns you.'

'You're right,' he agreed, 'but it interests me. The way you look, you certainly can't be short of men in your life.'

'The way I look generally attracts the wrong kind of men,' she said.

Dark brows lifted. 'What would you consider the right kind?'

'Those with a little more to them than an inflated income and an ego to match,' she retorted smartly. 'Money can't buy everything.'

'It can go a long way.' He ran a reminiscent gaze down the slender length of her body, returning to view her flushed cheeks and sparking eyes with a smile that made her want to kick him. 'Why are you really here, Alex?'

The question took her by surprise. It was an effort to keep her voice even. 'I'd have thought that was obvious.'

'Don't bother feeding me any ''had to see big brother again'' line. You neither of you come across as pining from lack of contact.'

'Perhaps because we're English, and the English don't parade their emotions. If I'd realised I was unwelcome,' she added tautly, 'I certainly wouldn't have come!'

Cal shook his head. 'I didn't say you were unwelcome, only that I doubted if the chance of seeing Greg again would be enough to bring you all the way out here. Hardly your scene, is it?'

'You've no idea what my scene might be!'

'I know what it isn't. You're as out of place on the Lazy Y as I would be in front of a camera!'

The way his chair was angled she was, to a certain extent, boxed into a corner, anything he said to her unlikely to be overheard above the general chatter. Done purposely? she wondered.

'If you're so perceptive,' she challenged, 'perhaps you'd like to take a guess at what other motive I *might* have had!'

'Running away from something, maybe.'

Her breath caught in her throat. He couldn't know, she reassured herself swiftly. The story was hardly of world interest. She conjured a laugh, hearing the brittle edge. 'And there I was congratulating myself on having committed the perfect crime!'

'Or someone,' he continued, as though she hadn't spoken. He gave her no time to form a response. 'What do you plan on doing with yourself while you *are* here? Your brother's going to be pretty busy.'

'Real or manufactured jobs?' Alex regretted the question the moment it was out, seeing the grey eyes suddenly harden, but it was too late to retract it. She made an effort to modify it instead. 'You seem to have been piling on the pressure a bit hard.'

'Been complaining, has he?'

'Not in so many words. More an impression I gathered.'

'You've been here all of three hours. You think that time enough to start making snap judgements?'

'I don't need to read a whole book to get an idea of the plot,' she countered, abandoning the pacification. 'I think you're probably giving Greg the run-around in the hope of showing him in his true colours—or what you consider his true colours. He's not the kind of husband you'd have chosen for Margot, is he?'

The hands had come down from behind the dark head, now, to rest on the arms of his chair, fingers curving the edge of the wood. Strong fingers, accustomed to controlling mettlesome horseflesh—among other things.

'If we're going in for plain speaking, no, he isn't,' came the blunt agreement. 'If she had to marry anybody this soon it should have been someone she knew something about.'

'Someone you already had in mind yourself, by any chance?'

'Someone *she* had in mind before meeting up with that brother of yours!'

Blue eyes clashed with grey, holding fast through sheer effort of will. 'Obviously not in any serious sense. If she's old enough to be married at all, she's old enough to make her own decisions.'

His lip curled. 'I guess you've been making yours most of your life!'

'Only since I realised it *was* my life.'

'Never made any mistakes?'

'Nothing radical.' It was a long way from the truth, but Alex was in no mood for ethical debate with herself. 'Anyway, it isn't me we're talking about.'

They were drawing attention, she realised, catching a couple of speculative glances. Her smile was purely for effect. 'I think we'd better leave it at that.'

Cal inclined his head. 'For now.' He got to his feet in one lithe movement, raising his voice to be heard over the others. 'Early start for those taking the all-day ride. Anybody not saddled up by six-thirty gets left behind!'

Groans greeted the announcement, though no one seemed seriously perturbed. To Alex, a full-day ride sounded tempting but, having not been on horseback for several weeks, she knew it would be wiser to harden up a little first. The last thing she needed was saddle-soreness.

In any case, she thought wryly, she hadn't been invited.

Cal went on indoors without a backward glance, leaving her to reflect on her lack of wisdom in calling him out the way she had. She hadn't set out with that intention. Not consciously, at any rate.

Wise or not, Alex was pretty certain she was right about his motives in putting Greg through the mill. He could even be hoping that, given enough of a hard time, his unwelcome brother-in-law would take off for pastures new. Greg's motives in marrying Margot might not be all they should be, but, the way she so obviously felt about him, she would be devastated if he did up and leave. That surely had to be taken into account.

Submerged in her thoughts, Alex started when one subject of them dropped into the chair recently vacated.

'Feeling the effects?' asked Margot sympathetically. 'I've never flown the Atlantic myself, but I can imagine what it's like to have all those hours' difference. What time will it be in England now?'

Glancing at the watch she had altered on the domestic flight from Denver, Alex did a quick calculation. 'Around five in the morning,' she hazarded, suddenly aware of it now. 'I've been on the go more than twenty-four hours!'

'Time you got some sleep, then, I'd think.'

Alex smiled at her. 'I think you're right. I want to be fresh for the morning.'

'Greg might not be around until evening, but I'll be here if you'd like some company.'

'I'd be glad of it. I've never been on a working ranch before. I've never been on any kind of ranch before, if it comes to that. It's all quite new to me.'

'You have some big farms in England, though, don't you? I'd have thought they were much the same kind of thing.'

'The biggest would hardly fill a corner of this spread. They don't use horses either—not for moving the cattle, at any rate. It's a whole different world.' Alex paused a moment, viewing the interest in the youthfully lovely face opposite. 'Greg must bring you over to visit,' she said on impulse. 'My flat isn't very big but we'd manage.'

'I'd love it!' Margot sounded genuinely enthusiastic. 'I always wanted to visit England.'

If Margot and Greg did come over, it was hardly going to be in the immediate future, Alex told herself. Time enough to get her life back in order first. Not that she imagined either of them would condemn her out of hand even if they did discover her secret. Cal was the only one likely to give no quarter.

She smothered an involuntary yawn with the back of her hand, aware of weariness infiltrating both body and mind. 'I'd better go on up before I fall asleep right here.'

'I'll come up with you,' said Margot. 'Nobody keeps late hours. Early morning is the best time of day.'

Alex could agree with that. She had never been one for sleeping in herself. A few hours' sleep and she would be ready to tackle anything—including Cal Forrester!

Others were already drifting away. Engrossed in conversation with one of the guests, Greg spared her the briefest attention when she paused to say goodnight.

'See you in a little while, honey,' he added to Margot,

at her back. 'Charlie's giving me the low-down on the insurance business.'

'Good line to be in,' said Charlie. 'Sure has been for me, at any rate. Way to go!'

For him, perhaps, Alex reflected, catching the expression in her brother's eyes and hoping he wasn't already contemplating a change of direction. Ranch life may not have turned out to be all he had anticipated, but the Lazy Y was Margot's home. Two months was hardly a fair trial, in any case.

She was reading too much into too little again, she chided herself, continuing on her way indoors. After eight years she could hardly hope to know her brother's mind on any level.

There was no sign of Cal inside. No sign of anyone, if it came to that. Margot said goodnight at the top of the stairs, looking, Alex thought, a little too determinedly cheerful. How many times, she wondered, had Greg left his wife to come to bed on her own like this?

'I'm really looking forward to seeing more of the ranch tomorrow,' she said. 'Perhaps we could take a ride together. Not too far, though,' she added laughingly. 'I need to take it in easy stages.'

'Right after breakfast,' Margot promised, obviously only too ready to fall in with whatever was proposed. 'I'm so glad you're here, Alex,' she added impulsively.

'So am I.' Alex leaned forward and placed a light kiss on her sister-in-law's cheek. 'See you in the morning. Bright and early!'

The door to Cal's room was firmly closed. Whether he was in there or not there was no way of knowing. If he was, and asleep already, it was unlikely that any small noise was going to waken him but, nevertheless, Alex

found herself tiptoeing around the bedroom as she un-
packed.

Would he sleep in pyjamas? she found herself wondering, and had a sudden vivid impression of that long,
lean body minus anything at all, bringing her to an
abrupt stop in the act of easing open a drawer to stow
away some clothing. She was hardly in the habit of indulging in lewd thoughts about men—for the most part
she preferred not to think of them at all these days—but
there was something about Cal Forrester that stirred her
baser instincts: something that liking had little to do
with.

Dangerous only if she allowed it to be, she told herself
hardily, stuffing undies into the half-open drawer, and
that she had no intention of doing.

She awoke to daylight and a feeling of well-being that
lasted only as long as it took her to register the position
of the hands on the bedside clock. Nine-thirty! The day
was half over!

Flinging back the bedclothes, she slid her feet into the
neat black mules she used as slippers and reached for
the light cotton wrap she had left over the end of the
bed. Breakfast would be long over by now, the all-day
party miles out on the trail. With any luck, Cal would
be off the homestead too. She would hate to face that
derisive smile of his when she finally got downstairs.

Showered, and dressed in jeans and blue chambray
shirt, she tied her hair back from her face with a pale
blue scarf and applied a hasty smear of lipstick before
leaving the room. Better late than never, she told herself,
but it wasn't convincing.

One of the youngish women who had served supper

was crossing the wide hall as Alex descended the stairs. She paused on sight of her.

'Didn't realise you were up yet,' she said without censure. 'What would you like for breakfast?'

'Just coffee will be fine, thanks,' Alex responded, unwilling to put the woman to any trouble when she must have other things to do. 'You're Janet, aren't you?'

'That's right. Janet Leeson. You can't go till lunchtime on just coffee,' she added. 'I'll fetch you some pancakes and syrup.'

'I'd be happier with toast,' Alex conceded. 'Quite happy to do it myself too. You don't have to wait on me.'

Janet lifted her shoulders in a cheerful shrug. 'It's what I'm paid for, honey. Anyway, Buck doesn't like folk invading his kitchen. You take yourself out on the veranda and I'll bring it to you. Too good a morning to hang about indoors.'

And had been for some time, thought Alex , ruefully, moving to obey the injunction as the older woman turned back the way she had come. At least she felt fully rested. After ten full hours' sleep she should do too!

There was no sign of Margot when she stepped onto the veranda. The mountains were etched against a sky of cobalt blue, the sun a blazing orb already high overhead. From the step she looked out over the corrals to the rolling grasslands beyond, glimpsing water through the belt of trees a quarter of a mile or so away. Having a river running right through Lazy Y land had to make it a particularly valuable property, she reckoned.

Life here must be pretty good all round, although the winters would be far more severe than anything she had ever experienced, with snow feet rather than mere inches deep. Even then there would be compensations such as skiing right on the doorstep, for instance. Not that she could ski, but given the incentive...

'So you made it,' commented a fast becoming familiar voice behind her, making muscle and sinew tense in involuntary response. 'Sleep well?'

Alex turned about slowly, maintaining a deadpan expression with the utmost difficulty. Dressed once more in jeans and shirt, thumbs hooked casually into his belt, one dark brow lifted in ironical enquiry, Cal leaned against the doorframe. How long had he been standing there watching her? she wondered fleetingly.

'Very well, thanks,' she said, determined not to show any discomfiture over her tardiness. 'I didn't expect to find you still around at this hour.'

'I had some paperwork to catch up on. There's more to raising cattle than riding herd.'

'I'm sure there is,' Alex returned smoothly. 'Just as there's more to modelling than standing in front of a camera.'

For a brief moment there was genuine humour in the grey eyes, then the mockery was back two-fold. 'I'll take your word for it. Have you eaten?'

'Janet is bringing me some toast and coffee,' she said, and felt herself moved to add, 'I'd have got it myself, but I understand your cook doesn't like strangers wandering about the kitchen.'

'Buck doesn't like *anybody* wandering about the kitchen,' Cal agreed. 'Including me.'

Alex lifted a brow in faithful imitation. 'You allow him to dictate?'

'Considering the difficulty I'd have in replacing him, I don't have much alternative.'

'Oh, well, I don't imagine you're all that eager to spend time in the kitchen anyway,' she said blandly.

'You could be right about that.' He came away from the doorjamb to allow Janet through, following her out to indicate the nearest group of chairs with a nod of his head. 'I'll join you.'

There were two cups already on the tray, Alex noted. Obviously Janet had anticipated some such move. She was none too keen on the idea herself, but she didn't have much alternative either.

Cal waited until she was seated before taking a seat himself, lifting both boot-clad feet to rest a heel on the rail with the ease of long custom.

'I wouldn't mind a piece of toast to go with it, if there's any going spare,' he said when Alex handed him a cup of the hot black coffee. 'Figuring always did work me up an appetite.'

'I'm surprised you don't employ an accountant,' she commented.

'I did at one time, until I found he was cheating me blind.'

Blue eyes lifted to regard the strongly carved features, taking in the firm line of his mouth, the hardness of jaw. 'What happened to him?'

'He spent some time behind bars.' The tone was matter-of-fact. 'He was lucky.'

'Meaning he might have got worse if he hadn't been locked up?'

'Meaning he was out inside a few months. We don't do any stringin' up these days.'

It was hardly what she had meant, but she let it pass. Chair tipped back, Cal looked in imminent danger of having it slide from under him, but she doubted if it would. Stretched out the way they were, and encased in close-fitting denim, his legs were long and straight, his thigh muscles clearly defined, his hips lean and hard.

There was no bulging of surplus flesh above the belt at his waist, just a broadening of frame to meet the wider line of his shoulders.

'Margot was going to show me round the place this morning,' she said on a somewhat edgy note. 'Have you seen her?'

'She's helping out over at the cabins,' he advised. 'One of the girls called in sick. I said I'd look after you till she's through.'

'You must have better things to do with your time.'

'Not especially. I'd hardly leave a guest to her own devices anyway.'

'I'm not a guest,' she pointed out. 'Not a paying one, at any rate. You don't have to entertain me.'

He flicked her a deceptively lazy glance, dwelling on the soft fullness of her mouth. 'Is that what I'm doing?'

Alex felt a sudden and unwelcome spiralling of heat from the pit of her stomach, the warmth running up under her skin as for a crazy moment she imagined what those lips of his would feel like on hers. She might not like the man but it had little bearing on her responses when he looked at her that way.

'Superbly,' she responded, emphasising the sarcasm in an effort to cover her confusion. 'The perfect host!'

'I'm gratified.' The expression in his eyes suggested an inner amusement. 'How much longer do you reckon on staying in the same line?'

The abrupt change of subject left her floundering again for a moment. She recovered with an effort, summoning a dismissive shrug. 'As long as the jobs keep coming in, I suppose.'

'And when they don't?'

'Something will turn up.'

'Or someone?'

It was all she could do to keep an even tone. 'Maybe even that. Providing it was the right someone.'

There was irony in his smile. 'True love or nothing, you mean? I didn't have you down for a romantic.'

'Just goes to show how wrong impressions can be. Maybe you're not quite the cynic you come across as either,' she added with deliberation. 'Could be I've totally misread your attitude where my brother's concerned.'

'An attitude based on two months' observation,' came the dry return. 'He's given me little reason to believe he cares for Margot the way she cares for him.'

The same doubt she had herself, Alex acknowledged wryly, but wasn't prepared to admit it.

'Few men wear their hearts on their sleeves,' she defended. 'That doesn't mean they don't feel anything. Greg wouldn't have married her if he didn't love her.'

'It's been eight years since the two of you were together,' Cal observed. 'Do you consider you still know him all that well?'

Alex bit her lip. 'People don't alter all that much.'

'Depends where they've been and who with. Eight years bumming round the world is hardly likely to strengthen character.'

'He had jobs,' she protested. 'He worked on an Australian sheep station, for one.'

'So he says.'

'It's true! He wrote to me from there.' Alex had no intention of admitting that it had been only the one letter. 'He was in a job when Margot met him, wasn't he?'

'Nightclub barman!' Cal made it sound like the lowest of the low. 'She didn't belong in any nightclub to start with.'

'So blame the people who took her there in the first place.'

'I do,' he said grimly. 'They won't be coming here again, that's for sure!'

Alex could hardly blame him for that—any more than she could blame him too much for failing to be over-joyed when his baby sister turned up with a husband in tow. In all fairness, she didn't see the present-day Greg as ideal husband material herself, but if he was what Margot wanted then it was surely best for her that every effort was made to keep the two of them together?

'Has it occurred to you,' she ventured, 'that if you did succeed in getting rid of Greg you might just finish up losing Margot too?'

'She wouldn't go with him.' It was a flat statement of fact.

'You mean you wouldn't allow it?'

'I mean I doubt very much that he'd want her to go with him.' He brought his feet down to the ground again, the chair back onto its four legs. 'If you've finished, we'll go fix you up with a horse.'

Alex replaced her empty cup in its saucer, aware of the futility in attempting to pursue the subject further. Not that there was a great deal more she could say on Greg's behalf, in any case. It was up to him to prove his own worth.

'I'm quite happy to wait until Margot's free,' she declared, reluctant to spend any more time in his company than she had to. 'In fact, I'd be more than happy to lend a hand.'

'Not necessary,' he said. 'But the offer's appreciated.'

Like hell! she thought sourly. Ten to one he took it for granted that she wouldn't know one end of a vacuum cleaner from another. If he had the same idea where horses were concerned, he was in for a surprise.

CHAPTER THREE

THERE were over a dozen animals in the corral, including the grey Alex recognised as the one Cal had ridden the previous evening. She settled her gaze on a deep-chested bay gelding restlessly pacing the perimeter fence.

'Is he available?' she asked, nodding in his direction.

'Available, yes,' Cal confirmed, 'but not suitable. The pinto is a good, smooth ride. Likewise the sorrel.'

'Suitable for a novice, maybe, but I *have* ridden before,' Alex returned firmly. 'The bay will suit me fine.'

'I said not.' The tone was level enough, but there was no doubting the determination.

Argument was obviously going to get her nowhere, she accepted with reluctance, squashing the urge. What was needed was a demonstration of her abilities.

'I'll take the chestnut mare over there, then,' she said, judging her the liveliest of the rest.

Cal inclined his head in mocking acknowledgement of her compromise. 'Let's go get a saddle.'

The tack room was at the end of the barn she had seen everyone making for last night, the tack itself in plentiful supply. Cal picked up a tooled leather saddle which looked twice the size of its English equivalent, dumping it into her arms with scant ceremony.

'Everybody does their own toting,' he notified her, hearing her involuntary gasp at the weight. 'Most folk like to stick to the same mount the whole time they're here.'

'I'd like to try different ones,' she said. 'If that's okay?'

The shrug was easy. 'Fine. Just stay away from the bay. He can be a cussed beggar when he has a mind.'

He wasn't the only one, thought Alex determinedly. She would ride that horse if it was the last thing she ever did!

The saddle grew heavier by the second as they made their way back across to the corral. She was thankful to sling it over the rail while Cal went in to put a bridle on the chestnut with a dexterity that thwarted her attempt to evade it. Hardly on a par with the bay, Alex considered, but at least not devoid of spirit.

She lofted the saddle over the gleaming back without waiting to be told, feeling the strain on her muscles. Talking softly to the animal, she reached for the girths, fastening them loosely at first, then taking up the slack when the deliberately drawn breath was released.

Ears pricking to the sound of her voice, the mare stood still as a rock as she gathered the reins in one hand and put a foot in the stirrup. A light bound and she was up and astride, settling down into the depths of the saddle with a lift of her eyebrows at the man watching.

'Feels fine,' she said. 'Like sitting in an armchair! I'm used to a lot less saddle than this.'

'A few less hours at a time in it too,' returned Cal drily. 'Walk her round a bit.'

She did so, enjoying the feel. 'What's her name?' she asked.

'Minty,' he supplied. 'Try a trot.'

Minty responded without hesitation to a touch of the heels. Using the Western-style one-handed hold on the reins, and refraining from rising, Alex found no difficulty in signalling changes of direction. She was show-

ing off a little, she knew, but it was time Cal realised
how far from a novice she actually was.

'Guess that's good enough,' he declared after a minute
or two.

Alex leaned forward to pat the silky neck as she
brought the mare to a halt, wryly accepting that that was
all she was going to get by way of approval. 'Any limitations on where I can go with her?'

'I'll be going into town this afternoon,' he said. 'You
can ride in with me. Don't bother putting the tack away,
Stick it on the rail over there.'

Alex sat where she was for a fuming moment as he
moved off back towards the house, strongly tempted to
take the bit between her own teeth. She had already
shown she could handle the animal; there was no call
for any further supervision!

Discretion beat rebellion into reluctant submission.
The fellowship between her and her sister-in-law's
brother was tentative, to say the least. Defiance of the
kind she was contemplating was hardly scheduled to im-
prove things. Like it or not, while she was here on the
Lazy Y, what he said went.

Having arrived on the scene in time to hear the edict,
Margot grinned as she dismounted, obviously aware of
the brief struggle. 'I half expected you to take off regardless,' she commented.

'He's the boss,' Alex responded lightly, unbuckling
the girths. 'I wouldn't mind seeing the town anyway.
How far is it?'

'A few miles. Not that it's anything like what you're
used to.'

Alex glanced at the younger girl, struck by a certain
disparagement in her voice. 'I'd be very disappointed if
it were. You'll be coming along too, won't you?'

Margot shook her head. 'I've one or two things I need to do this afternoon.'

Which left *her* well and truly saddled, Alex thought ruefully, bracing herself for the descending weight.

Turned back into the corral, Minty kicked up her heels, as if in protest at the re-confinement. Alex knew how she felt. A good gallop across the wide open expanses out there would have done them both the world of good.

'I always envied the girls at school who had ponies of their own,' she said, reluctant to leave the animals. 'I'd have been in seventh heaven living your kind of life, Margot!'

Slender shoulders rose in deprecation. 'I'd be the same if I had *your* life. Going on shoots, wearing glamorous clothes—seeing all those places! Before that trip to Vegas the farthest I'd been was Denver. I thought being married would make things different,' she added, 'but it hasn't. Not really. I'm still stuck in the same rut.'

Alex looked at her thoughtfully. 'Does Cal know how you feel?'

She shook her head. 'I didn't realise what I was missing myself until I went to Vegas. There was so much to do—so many places to go!'

'All of it costing money,' Alex said softly. 'You must have realised Greg didn't have very much.'

'I didn't think about it,' Margot admitted. 'We had such a wonderful time together.'

Alex could imagine. With just the one week in which to secure his future, Greg would have pulled out all the stops. It must have been a real shock when he had met his brother-in-law and realised just how far from Easy Street he'd landed himself.

She was doing it again, she acknowledged ruefully,

pulling herself up. She had no real proof, as yet, of what Greg's motives had been.

'Do you love him?' she asked, and saw the hazel eyes take on a glow.

'Oh, yes!' The glow faded again. 'I don't think he loves me, though. Not in the same way.'

'Men don't always find it easy to demonstrate their feelings, but I'm sure he does.' Alex did her best to infuse certainty into her voice. 'Why else would he have been so eager for me to come and meet you?'

'I suppose you're right.' Margot was obviously eager to be convinced. 'I'm probably expecting too much.' She paused. 'Have you ever been in love yourself?'

Alex summoned a smile, a lightness of tone. 'I'm still waiting for the bells to ring.'

'But you must have met a lot of terrific men!'

'Not ones likely to offer the kind of relationship I'm looking for.'

'You mean marriage?'

'Possibly. Something lasting, at any rate.'

'The way you feel about this kind of life, you and Cal would be well suited.'

Alex cracked a laugh. 'Like chalk and cheese!'

'A whole lot better than him and Diane,' Margot continued, ignoring the irony. 'She's nowhere near as nice as you are. Nowhere near as good-looking either.'

'Well, thanks.' Alex was watching the bay, admiring his powerful conformation. 'Who is she?'

'Joss Lattimer's daughter. He owns the Circle X.'

'They have an understanding, do they?'

'Diane would like to think they have.' Margot wrinkled her nose. 'I'd hate to have *her* as a sister-in-law.'

'Well, if she's what Cal wants...' Alex turned away

from the fence, dismissing the subject from her mind. 'You were going to show me round.'

They spent the next hour looking over the homestead. Log-built, the six guest cabins were self-contained and comfortably furnished, two of them capable of sleeping four people if required, although the majority apparently came in pairs and sometimes even singly. They were heated by wood-burning stoves in the winter when people came to ski and sleigh-ride, with Calor gas fires as stand-bys for the cool summer evenings. Alex would have been quite content to live in one of them the whole year round.

The bunk house, over beyond the barn, was for the single hands only, the married ones coming in on a daily basis. Most were out on jobs at present, two of them with Greg, line-riding the fences to check for breakages.

'The Circle X lost about thirty head to rustlers last week,' Margot said. 'They back a truck into the fence to break a section down, and use dogs to bring in as many as they can. Cal set a trap last year and put one gang out of circulation for a while, but that didn't deter the others for long. It's too lucrative a game.'

'What kind of a trap?' Alex asked, intrigued to hear that rustling actually still took place.

'He put a bunch of prime steers where they could be easily got at, then lay in wait with several of the boys every night for more than a week waiting for them.'

'But how could he be sure they'd come? I mean, if they didn't know the cattle were there...'

'They send spotters out looking for likely prospects. They must have thought they'd got it made.'

'They were all caught?'

'Every one. Got twelve months apiece. If it had been up to Cal, it would have been twelve years!'

Alex didn't doubt it. She could visualise the scene in her mind's eye: the men lying in wait in the night; the truck coming into view, engine muffled as horses' hooves might once have been; the sudden commotion as the ambush was sprung. In former days, the thieves might have found themselves strung up on the spot. A few months in jail hardly carried the same deterrent value.

With all the guests on the day-ride, and Greg still out, it was just the three of them for lunch on the veranda. Remembering the amount of food available at supper, Alex conserved her appetite. She might have given up modelling but that was no excuse for gorging herself.

'You don't eat enough to keep a sparrow alive!' scoffed Cal, watching her quarter an apple for dessert. 'A few extra pounds wouldn't hurt.'

'Alex has an absolutely perfect figure now,' declared his sister with some asperity. 'I wish I could look like she does!'

'You'd need stretching a few inches to start with,' he said. 'Plus a bleach-job on the hair.'

'What time did you intend leaving?' asked Alex, judging it better to change the subject than go for his guts.

'As soon as we're through.' From the glint in his eyes, he was well aware of her irritation. 'You might find a hat useful. Keep the sun out of your eyes.'

'I've got several,' Margot offered. 'You're welcome to borrow one.'

Alex smiled at her. 'Thanks. I'll probably buy myself one as a souvenir to take home.'

The hazel eyes took on a sudden concern. 'You don't have to go soon, do you?'

It was difficult to know quite how to answer that without appearing to take too much for granted. 'I don't have anything particularly pressing lined up,' she acknowledged diffidently.

'Slack time of year, is it?' Cal gave her no time to answer the question. 'There's no limit this end on how long you stay.'

'Thanks,' she said again. 'That's very generous of you.'

His lips slanted. 'It's no hardship. You might like to join in some of the guest activities. There's a cookout tomorrow night, and the Prescott rodeo on Saturday, with a square dance in the evening.'

'What about general ranch work?' she asked. 'Greg said the guests joined in with that too.'

'Some of the men like to put in a spell or two.'

'Women barred, are they?'

Cal eyed the bright cascade of her hair, freed now from its tethering scarf, the fine boning of her features; dropping his gaze to view her well-tended hands with obvious implication. 'It's no job for a woman.'

'Where I come from,' she said with purpose, 'women are deemed capable of doing anything they feel capable of doing!'

'Always providing they don't overestimate their capabilities.'

'The proof of the pudding is in the eating. I already showed you I can sit a horse.'

'Think you could use a rope too?'

'I could learn.'

The smile was tolerant. 'I'll consider it.' He pushed back his chair and got to his feet, tall, dark and infuriating. 'See you down at the corral in ten minutes.'

Margot chuckled at the expression on Alex's face as her brother moved away. 'You look as if you'd like to stick a knife in his back!'

'More than one!' Alex caught herself up. 'Sorry about that. He *is* your brother.'

'You don't need to apologise. He makes me just as mad at times. You do realise he was needling you on purpose?'

Alex looked at her sharply, then gave a rueful smile. 'You mean he does let the women take part?'

'If they show any real enthusiasm.'

'I thought that was what I was doing.'

Margot hesitated. 'Don't take this the wrong way, but you hardly look the type to enjoy roughing it.'

'Never judge a book by its cover.' Alex stood up purposefully. 'I'll just have to prove myself, won't I?'

Cal had both horses already tacked-up when she reached the corral. Seated easily astride the grey, one hand on the rein, the other resting lightly along his thigh, he looked born to the saddle—the embodiment of all the cowboy heroes Alex had worshipped as a child. Not unlike them in essence either, she supposed: the all-male male in a male-dominated world. Fine enough in fiction, maybe, but downright insufferable in reality!

'Glad to see you remembered the hat,' he said. 'Fit you okay?'

'It's a bit snug,' she admitted. 'Shall I be able to get one of my own this afternoon?'

'Don't see why not.' He pulled his own hat further down over his eyes as he set the grey into motion with a flick of the rein. 'Let's get on the way.'

Regardless of the company, Alex found it impossible to feel anything but elated as they moved out under the wide blue Wyoming sky. It was all she had anticipated: the sun hot, the air clear, the scenery awesome in its beauty. What more could Greg want from life? she wondered. What more could anyone want? If she never saw a city street again she wouldn't care!

There wasn't much chance of that, of course. She might stretch this to a couple of weeks, but she had to go back some time. Whether she would take the job she had been offered she hadn't yet decided. They had given her a month to think about it, and she had money put by, so the decision wasn't pressing, although she could hardly afford to be choosy. Considering the kind of publicity she'd been given, she was lucky to have the opportunity at all.

They were heading towards the river along a well-used trail. Minty was full of running; she could feel it in her. Time to show what she was made of once and for all, she thought recklessly, abandoning the soul-searching. She gave the mare her head, feeling the surging power in the silken muscles as they leapt straight into full gallop.

Cal shouted something as she passed him, but she paid no heed, urging Minty on to even greater efforts in the certainty that he would come after her. If nothing else, she could give him a run for his money!

The grey was right alongside when she finally pulled up on reaching the belt of pine trees edging the river. Eyes sparkling, hat flung to the back of her head, she directed a challenging smile at the man astride the other horse.

'Ready to grant me full membership now?'

'Do that again,' he said hardily, 'and I'll ground you for the duration!'

Alex lifted her eyebrows in mock surprise. 'You wanted to know if I could handle her, didn't you?'

'Not at the risk of you breaking your neck!'

'I was never in any danger of falling off. It's just about impossible from these saddles!'

'Don't count on it. If she'd put a foot in a hole—' Cal broke off, looking as if tolerance had just about reached its limits. 'You'll do as you're damned well told!'

'Temper!' she admonished. 'You're scaring the horses.'

A spark leapt in the grey eyes. Without appearing to give any direction to the animal beneath him he closed the gap between them, leaning across to thrust a hand into the thickness of hair at her nape and yank her bodily towards him. It was hardly the first time she'd been kissed, but never quite like this, she thought dazedly. She could feel the hard pressure of his thigh against hers, smell the emotive masculine scent of his skin. Her response was involuntary, governed by some deep-down, almost primitive instinct she couldn't have controlled if she'd tried.

She was breathless when he finally let her go, struggling to contain herself.

'You may be able to play that game back home and get away with it,' he said with deliberation, 'but try it with me again and you might finish up with more than you bargained for!'

'Game!' The word almost choked her. 'If you think I'd—'

'Spare me the outraged heroine act!' he cut in derisively. 'You've been kissed before.'

'If I have, it's been with a little finesse!' she got out. 'The macho tactics might impress the women round here, but they don't impress me!'

His sudden grin was a taunt in itself. 'I didn't notice all that much resistance.'

'I wouldn't demean myself by struggling with an oaf like you!' Alex caught herself up as she saw the grin widen, aware of sounding like the outraged heroine he had already mentioned. 'Are we going into town or aren't we?' she added tersely.

The smile still plucking at his lips, Cal inclined his head. 'Just make sure you behave yourself from now on.'

He put the grey into motion with a touch of the rein against the strong neck, leaving Alex to follow on behind with a yen to throw something hard and heavy at the arrogant dark head. The scene they'd just played could have come pretty much verbatim from any one of a dozen or more old films she remembered, but Cal was no celluloid hero. Considering the way she'd responded to him just now, it would be wise to make sure she didn't provoke any further demonstrations. She wouldn't put anything past *this* man!

They crossed the river at a narrow ford, the horses hock-deep in the swiftly moving water. Alex left it to the mare to pick her own route, thankful to get out the other side without a stumble.

Cloud was beginning to pile up over the mountains, she saw, glancing across when they reached the top of the wooden slope, although the sky still stretched an unbroken blue overhead.

'Are we in for some rain?' she asked, deciding to put the whole episode aside.

'Could be,' Cal answered. 'We get a lot of summer storms.' He looked her way, expression difficult to define. 'Not afraid of thunder, are you?'

'Not up to now,' she said. 'On the other hand, I've never been out on horseback in a storm.'

'We'll be back before it gets here. I don't plan on spending long in town.'

Meaning she'd better not plan on it either, Alex assumed. No big deal, she told herself firmly, clamping down on the mutinous streak as it stirred to life once more; she could always come in again.

'I take it I *will* be allowed out on my own after this?' she said, doing her best to oust any hint of sarcasm.

'No reason why not,' he agreed. 'You've given a fair account of yourself.'

Alex winged a suspicious glance at him, but there was no sardonic tilt to the strong mouth. 'I've been riding since I was seven,' she affirmed, electing to take the comment at face value.

'Your own pony?'

She shook her head regretfully. 'Just a couple of times a week at the local stables—more when I was old enough to go up in the evenings and at weekends to help out.'

'Was Greg enthusiastic about horses, too?'

'Not to the same degree.'

'But the two of you were close as children?'

'Very.' Alex hesitated, not really sure if this was the right time to try putting her brother's case again—not all that sure what else she *could* say.

Cal took the decision out of her hands. 'I'm not prepared to go over the same ground again, if that's what you're considering,' he stated unequivocally. 'So don't waste your breath.'

'The way you feel about Greg, I find it difficult to understand why you allowed him to invite me here at all,' she said after a moment or two. 'After all, we're out of the same mould.'

'It was Margot's idea to ask you over—when he finally got around to telling her he had a sister. Up until then she'd believed he was all alone in the world.'

Alex bit her lip. 'Perhaps he just wanted time to adjust first.' It sounded lame to her own ears; it was no surprise to see Cal's scornful expression. She added staunchly, 'Whatever his reasons, it doesn't matter now, does it?'

'Obviously not to you,' he said.

It mattered a lot, but she had no intention of letting Greg down by revealing it.

They were descending into another wide valley with a cluster of buildings that must be Prescott discernible on the far side. About another twenty minutes' riding at the pace they were going, she reckoned. The cloud was still building up behind them, but no doubt Cal knew what he was talking about when he said they had plenty of time.

She stole a glance at the hard-hewn profile, feeling a sudden tremor run the length of her spinal column at the memory of how that mouth of his had felt on hers. How would it feel, she wondered, to have him kiss her because he wanted to rather than as retribution for her taunting?

She'd do best to forget that line of thought, she told herself roughly. No good could come of it.

CHAPTER FOUR

BUT for one or two motor vehicles parked at the curbside, the twentieth century hadn't made all that much of an impact on the town, Alex was glad to see. Judging from the hitching rails *in situ* outside several of the buildings down the tree-lined main street, horses still played a major role in transportation.

Cal dismounted at one shop-fronted edifice bearing the legend COUNTY SHERIFF on its windows.

'I'll be a few minutes,' he said. 'You might like to have a look round while you wait.'

Alex watched him stride indoors, unable to deny that every movement of that lean, fit body sent quivers running through her. Physical attraction played havoc with the senses, she acknowledged ruefully. Not a lot she could do about it except ride it out.

If he was only going to be a few minutes there obviously wasn't going to be time to explore very far. She stayed with the horses instead, rubbing Minty's soft nose while keeping a wary eye on the grey, who was doing a lot of snorting and head-tossing. Trust Cal to choose to ride a stallion, she thought with irony.

Attention occupied, she hardly noticed the Land Rover pulling in nearby. Only when the driver got out and moved towards her did she turn a glance, seeing a young woman dressed much the same way as she was herself.

'That's Cal Forrester's horse, so I guess you must be

Alex,' said the newcomer. 'I'm Diane Lattimer from the Circle X.'

Alex had somehow known it. Not that Margot had done the girl full justice in the looks department, she reflected, viewing the dark hair curling softly about the strikingly attractive face, the unusual amber eyes. Diane could have made a very good living in her own line.

'Hi,' she returned. 'Nice to meet you. Cal's inside, but he shouldn't be long.'

'Then I'll wait. I was coming over to see him anyway.' Diane leaned against the rail, ignoring the restless grey. 'How long are you here for?'

Too long, if that underlying tone was anything to go by, Alex conjectured; it was by no means the first time she had heard it. She wouldn't have had Diane down as the type to fear competition, even where there might be some.

'Probably just a couple of weeks,' she said, and saw a flash of something approaching relief in the amber eyes.

'Just a vacation, then?'

What else could she have thought it might be? wondered Alex fleetingly.

'That's right,' she confirmed. 'A chance to see my brother again. You've met Greg, I suppose?'

'Sure. He's quite a guy!'

Alex retained a level note with some difficulty, by no means deaf to the nuances. 'Margot obviously thinks so.'

'Margot was always impressionable,' came the smooth rejoinder. 'Not that anybody expected her coming back from Vegas with a husband in tow!'

'Life holds a lot of surprises,' Alex commented lightly, determined not to be drawn.

'Some greater than others,' agreed Cal, emerging from

the office in time to hear the last remark. He gave Diane a smile lacking in the mockery Alex was accustomed to. 'What brings you into town?'

The answering smile was bright and warm and, to Alex at least, overdone. 'I was on my way to your place when I saw Jed tied up. You don't usually ride in.'

'Depends how much time I've got,' he said easily. 'Anything special you wanted to see me about?'

'I was wondering if you were entered for the rodeo Saturday, that's all.'

A question she could have asked over the phone, Alex surmised, and wondered if the same thought had occurred to Cal.

'I'm down,' he confirmed. 'How about you?'

'Oh, definitely!' She turned a somewhat condescending glance back in Alex's direction. 'I guess you don't have rodeos where you come from?'

'We have gymkhanas,' Alex replied blandly. 'Much the same thing.'

Cal's lips twitched. 'You wanted to look for a better-fitting hat, didn't you?' he asked.

'Well…yes.' She was thrown for a moment. 'But I thought you were in a hurry to get back?'

'I can spare another ten minutes.' He gave Diane another of the amiable smiles. 'See you Saturday.'

Seeing the look in the amber eyes as he turned away, Alex felt a sudden pang of sympathy for the girl. Whatever Cal's feelings for her might be, they were apparently nowhere near as potent as hers for him.

'Does Circle X land touch on yours at all?' she queried when they were out of earshot.

'It's the next ranch east of the Lazy Y,' he confirmed. 'Why?'

Her shrug was thoughtful. 'I'd have thought a merger would be advantageous.'

'Not enough to tempt me into marrying for the sake of it, if that's what you're getting at.'

'You could do a lot worse than Diane.'

'I'm sure I could.' Brow lifted sardonically, he glanced down at her. 'You only just met her. Why the interest?'

'I was thinking that marriage might mellow you a little,' she returned with honeyed sweetness. 'The love of a good woman, and all that!'

His mouth widened briefly. 'I doubt if Diane would appreciate being seen as a mellowing influence, but I'll bear the recommendation in mind if and when I get round to considering marriage at all.'

'Leave it too long and you might find yourself short on choice,' she said, and drew another taunting glance.

'I'll take the chance.'

With small risk of finding himself left on the shelf, Alex conceded. Diane was probably only one of many who would like to land the boss of the Lazy Y.

Finding a hat to fit was no problem, choosing a shape and colour something else again. Determined not to be rushed, despite Cal's growing impatience, she tried on over a dozen before finally settling on a creamy beige one with a black band. She would have liked a pair of the tooled leather boots too, but decided enough was enough for one day.

Even then, the stipulated ten minutes had stretched closer to twenty-five by the time they emerged onto the street again. Alex was both surprised and a little perturbed to see how far the cloud had extended. Dark and threatening, it covered almost a third of the blueness. A flash of lightning over the mountains was followed just a few seconds later by the rumble of thunder, fairly distant at present but obviously coming this way.

'Are we going to make it back before it breaks?' she asked as they mounted the horses, trying not to reveal any concern.

Cal shrugged. 'If we don't, we get wet.'

At least this time she'd be fully clothed, she consoled herself.

The sun was still shining when they reached the top of the ridge. Watching the cloud-bank's advance, Alex calculated that they might have just enough time to make the ranch before it spread overhead and released whatever load it was carrying. The thunder was certainly closer, the lightning spectacular. It would be dangerous, down on the range, if the cattle she could see bunching in the near distance were panicked by it into stampeding.

Cal was looking that way too, but skywards, not down. Following his gaze, Alex focused on several circling black dots which resolved themselves into birds of some kind.

'Buzzards?' she hazarded, and he looked at her in surprise.

'How did you know that?'

'Films I've seen. There's something dead down there, isn't there?'

'Something pretty big to attract that many,' he agreed. 'I'll come back and check on it later.'

'What's wrong with now?' she countered, seized by an urge to show her true mettle. 'It isn't that much of a detour.'

The grey eyes appraised her narrowly for a moment, as if calculating her seriousness. 'Far enough to make it unlikely we'd beat the storm.'

'So what's a little rain?' she said carelessly. 'I've been

wet before.' She put Minty into motion with a touch of
her heels against the smooth sides, turning a deaf ear to
any cautioning voices. 'Let's go!'

Cal followed in her wake, only moving up to take the
lead when they reached the bottom of the incline and
passed through the gate onto Lazy Y land, heading for
the spot where the buzzards were still circling. Only
three of them now, Alex counted, which meant the rest
were probably on the ground tearing at the carcass that
had drawn them there. Whatever it was, it wouldn't be
a pretty sight.

It hadn't looked all that far from the ridge, but even
at a canter it took them several minutes to reach the spot.
Although several of the big birds flapped into the air on
their approach, a couple remained where they were, rip-
ping out great chunks of the already half-eaten steer with
powerful beaks.

They flew up when Cal shouted, but sluggishly, as if
their stomachs were too full for proper take-off, an impression confirmed when the pair of them landed a short
distance away and commenced patrolling back and forth,
as if waiting for the unwelcome newcomers to depart
again. Ugly creatures, with their hairless red heads and
necks, thought Alex with a shudder, keeping a wary eye
on them as she dismounted. Not that they were likely to
attack live humans, she supposed.

The steer was relatively fresh, from the look of it,
although the smell was already bad enough to make her
nose wrinkle. Both hindquarters were missing. Hacked
with some sharp instrument rather than torn away, it appeared. Hardly the work of an animal, then.

'Rustlers?' she asked.

'Itinerants short on food, at a guess. We get a lot
coming through in search of work.' Cal straightened

from his examination, tipping his hat back to gaze across the quarter-mile of grassland separating them from the general herd. 'A stray this close to the fence would be an easy shot.'

'But why only take the hindquarters?'

'Takes time to butcher a whole steer. They wouldn't want to risk being seen by any night watch.'

'You're taking it all so calmly!' Alex exclaimed, viewing the clean-cut profile. 'Aren't you furious?'

'No point getting het-up about it,' he returned. 'Whoever they are, they'll probably be long gone by now, but I'll get Taylor to keep an eye open, just in case they are still hanging around.'

Taylor, Alex assumed, was the County Sheriff just visited. Maybe the modern West was different in many ways from the cinema depiction, but the basic flavour was the same. All it needed at the moment was for a group of Indians to come whooping round the shoulder of the hill to complete the picture!

She had totally forgotten the weather during the last fifteen minutes or so. The huge spots of rain she felt splash on the crown of her hat wiped all flights of fancy from mind.

'Better get mounted,' Cal advised. 'It's going to come heavy.'

That, thought Alex, as the heavens literally opened moments later, had to be classed as the understatement of the year! Within seconds she was soaked to the skin, shirt flattened to her body, water dripping from her hat-brim and running down the slope of the saddle to reach even the unexposed areas, jeans clinging damply to her thighs. She was only thankful that Minty seemed impervious to the onslaught, although the sheer force of the rain had to be stinging her hide.

No better off than she was, Cal seemed impervious too, riding tall in the saddle at her side, tanned features expressing no particular emotion. It had been her own suggestion that they make the detour, Alex reminded herself, reluctant to let the side down by allowing her own decidedly less stoic emotions to show. At least it was warm rain. Back home she would probably have been frozen to the marrow by now!

After one great clap, almost directly overhead, the thunder gradually decreased in volume, fading away south. A line of blue appeared over the mountain range, widening by the minute as the storm clouds moved on to fresh pastures. The rain stopped as suddenly as it had begun, the re-emerging sun drawing immediate steam from wet hides.

Alex eased her damp upper leg away from the saddle leather, grimacing at the feel of it. 'Did you say you get a lot of summer storms?'

'Fifty or sixty some years,' Cal confirmed.

'That's worse than back home!'

'With the difference that we see a lot more of the sun, from all I've heard. You'll soon dry off,' he added, with what she considered a total lack of appreciation for her fortitude. 'There'll be plenty of time to pretty yourself up before supper.'

Forgetting the discomfort, she turned a sparkling blue gaze towards him. 'You really think the way I look is *all* I care about?'

'Maybe not *all*,' came the unmoved return, 'but a great part. Your looks are your stock-in-trade, aren't they?'

'I do happen to have a brain too!'

'For what use you make of it.'

Alex drew in a long, slow breath, fighting to control

her uncivilised urges. If ever a man needed kicking where it hurt, he was it! Not that she was in any position to deliver—or he to receive, for that matter.

'You've no idea what my job entails,' she rejoined with what restraint she could manage. 'How would you like to spend hours under roasting arc lights, conjuring up expressions and poses to order, or model beachwear out in the open in the middle of winter and make it look as if you're having the greatest time on earth?'

'That takes stamina, not intelligence,' he said, unimpressed. 'And if you don't enjoy it, why continue doing it?'

'I'm not', it was on the tip of her tongue to say. She bit it back with an effort, unwilling to give that much away, lifting her shoulders in a brief shrug. 'It pays well.'

His lips acquired a cynical twist. 'Last night you said money wasn't everything.'

'What I actually said was it can't *buy* everything,' she corrected. 'I dare say I could find a man to keep me if I were willing to play that kind of game, but—'

'But as you said earlier, you're looking for love,' he finished for her. 'Aren't we all?'

'I'd doubt if it was *your* main priority,' she retorted.

'You know me so well already?'

The irony renewed the spark in her eyes. 'It doesn't take any great insight to recognise misanthropy!'

His laugh riled her all the more. 'There might be one or two people I take exception to, but I'd say I was reasonably tolerant about the rest.'

'My brother being one of the two, of course,' she said tartly.

The lean features hardened, humour banished. 'I said I wasn't prepared to discuss it any further.'

'But you're still hoping he'll take off if you make things difficult enough for him!' Alex was too angry to take any heed of the flat statement. 'You're a bigot through and through!'

'I judge as I find,' he returned grimly. 'And I'm finding *you* a major irritation right now! Just stow it, will you?'

Nothing she said was going to make any difference anyway, Alex told herself, swallowing any further invective. Greg probably wouldn't thank her for sticking her oar in either. If it weren't for her liking Margot so much, she might seriously consider heading straight back home again.

She was lying to herself, and she knew it. She had far more selfish reasons for wanting to stay. Cal and summer storms notwithstanding, this place was still her personal Valhalla—the nearest to heaven on earth she was ever likely to come. If only she *never* had to go back!

Expression controlled, Cal put the grey into a canter, a move followed immediately by Minty with no urging from Alex. She let the mare have her way, only too eager to get this journey over as quickly as possible.

They reached the ranch to find the guest group already in the process of unsaddling their mounts. They'd been caught in the downpour too, but no one seemed particularly concerned.

'I see you had the boss all to yourself,' commented the woman who had spent the whole of supper the previous evening commandeering Cal's attention as Alex unsaddled Minty close by. 'Lucky girl!'

Alex kept her tone easy. 'Aren't I just? And how was your day?'

'An experience not to be missed if you get the chance while you're here. They do the mountain ride every week. I wouldn't mind staying on another week myself,' she added, 'but Fred has to be back in the office Monday. At least we'll be here for the rodeo Saturday. That should really be worth watching! Some of the Lazy Y boys are taking part—including Cal, too, I'd think. I hear he's won prizes for bronco riding.'

No surprises there, Alex reflected drily. Horse breaking was just about his metier!

Jed was back in the corral already, his owner on the way to the barn with two of the other men, the heavy saddle no problem to him. Strong as an ox and unyielding as a rock, that was Cal Forrester. Any woman who felt the way Diane Lattimer obviously did about him must be an out-and-out masochist!

Greg was back too, she learned from one of the other wranglers. As Margot didn't appear to be around, she could hope that the two of them were enjoying a little time alone together. Their bedroom door was closed when she went upstairs, though that in itself meant nothing, she supposed.

The new hat looked a great deal less pristine than it had in the shop, after its soaking, but it still retained its shape. Which was more than could be said for her hair, Alex thought wryly, running her fingers through the damp, flattened tresses in a vain attempt to give it back some lift. If she went down to supper with it like this it would certainly be one in the eye for Cal and his theory that her looks were all-important to her—but then why should she care *what* he believed? There was nothing whatsoever wrong with wanting to look one's best.

Whether it was the fresh air or the exercise, or a combination of both, she found herself with a very much sharpened appetite at supper, followed by a lazy disinclination to do anything at all afterwards.

A day spent in the saddle had many of the guests smothering yawns before the evening was very far gone. Most were intending to take it easy the next day, although a couple of the men planned on joining the workforce. Gluttons for punishment, declared Greg.

If Cal heard the comment, he ignored it. Apart from an ironical glance at the newly washed hair, he more or less ignored Alex too. Still finding her an irritation, she assumed. Well, that cut both ways!

Happily, Greg appeared to be paying his wife more attention tonight. Margot blossomed under it like a flower beneath the sun, eyes sparkling, laughter never very far from her lips. Watching the two of them, Alex was pretty certain that she had misjudged her brother's motives to a great extent. Maybe he had seen an opportunity to make a new life for himself, but that wasn't to say he didn't care for Margot. What man could fail to care for someone so utterly delightful both in looks *and* personality?

Of them all, only Cal looked on the pair with cynicism. But then, he looked on love itself with cynicism. He'd probably never marry, because he'd never allow any woman that much of a hold over him. A psychologist would say there had to be reasons in his past for that kind of attitude. Perhaps he'd been badly let down by some woman and wasn't prepared to take the risk of it happening again.

Amateur analysis based on pure speculation, she admonished herself derisively at that point. He'd probably been born a cynic!

Afraid of oversleeping again, she found sleep difficult to come by at all. When she did finally drift off, it was to dream of riding a stuffed horse that gradually came apart in the rain, leaving her stranded in a pile of straw that turned to bones and brought hundreds of hungry vultures swooping down on her out of a sky the colour of blood.

Waking with a thumping heart to early-morning light, she knew a very real relief. What a psychologist might make of that little lot, she hated to think!

It was only just gone four-thirty, but she knew she wouldn't sleep again now. Slipping on a pair of jeans and a sweater, she crept downstairs and out onto the veranda, shivering a little in the crisp, high range air. There was no one else about as yet, nor probably would there be for another hour or so. Time and to spare for what she had in mind.

The bay was among the dozen or so horses left overnight in the nearest of the corrals. He eyed her suspiciously as she made her way towards him with the halter she had fetched from the barn, snorting and backing when she put out a hand, but settling down again as she spoke softly and reassuringly to him, allowing her to slide the bit between his teeth with only a token protest.

So much for Cal's cautionary tales, Alex thought scathingly, leading the animal from the corral. She'd known riding-stable horses who were more trouble than this!

The early morning was the best time of all to ride— although she'd never been out quite as early before, she had to admit. She looked forward to seeing Cal's face when she dropped it out at the breakfast table. Maybe after this he'd stop treating her like a greenhorn!

The bay was bigger than Minty, but she managed to hoist the saddle without too much difficulty and fasten the girths with no more than the usual resistance. Piece of cake! she exulted, swinging herself up.

The truth in the saying that pride went before a fall

was brought home to her with emphasis as the bay suddenly bucked. Taken completely unawares, she grabbed at the horn, the breath jerked out of her as he did it again.

Anger overcame shock. The damned animal wasn't going to get the better of her if she could help it! Digging her knees in, she rode out the next couple of jolts, every bone in her body jarred by the impact, teeth feeling as if they were coming loose from their sockets.

As though in recognition of a bloody-mindedness equal to his own, the gelding stopped as suddenly as he had begun, swinging his head round to eye her with such a comical air of surprise that she had to laugh, despite her aches and pains.

'You don't get rid of *me* that easy!' she confirmed. 'We're going for a ride, like it or not!'

Keeping him under firm control, she turned him towards the main gate, heart performing a painful double beat as Cal moved out from the shadows to block her progress.

'You're not going anywhere,' he stated. 'Not on that horse.'

Alex set her jaw, prepared this time to make a fight of it. 'You've obviously been there long enough to see me master him, so what's the problem?' she demanded. 'Piqued because I disobeyed orders?'

The muscles around the strong mouth tautened ominously. 'I'm not arguing with you,' he said with the same flat intonation. 'You either get down, or I fetch you down. Your choice.'

He moved swiftly forward as he saw the sudden flare in her eyes, grasping the rein close up by the bit to hold the animal in check. 'Try it, and you'll rue it,' he warned.

Considering the conflict going on around him, the bay

was showing remarkably little disturbance. About as dangerous as a Shetland pony! Alex thought furiously, refusing to acknowledge that Cal might be the calming influence himself.

'A real John Wayne line!' she mocked, making no move to obey. 'You should be in the movies!'

'Wayne would have had you down and across his knee by now,' came the caustic return. 'Maybe not a bad idea!'

Discretion was the better part of valour, Alex reminded herself, biting back an equally caustic retort. She wouldn't put it past him to follow through on that particular notion.

'Maybe we should both be in the movies,' she suggested, giving way to sudden humour. 'Me the tempestuous heroine, you the masterful hero. Typecasting all the way!'

Amusement took over from ire in the grey eyes, his mouth pulling into an unwilling smile. 'I'll give you masterful hero if you don't get down from there!'

Defused but by no means diverted, Alex reflected wryly. She brought a leg over to slide reluctantly to the ground, smoothing a hand down the muscular neck. 'Seems we're to be kept apart after all, boy.'

'For your own good.' Cal sounded reasonably tolerant again. 'You handled him okay just now, but that doesn't make him a safe bet for a lone ride over country you don't even know.'

'If he's such an unpredictable character, why do you keep him at all?' she asked.

'Because he *is* a character—as well as being one of the best cow ponies going when he's in the mood.' He lifted an interrogative eyebrow as she continued to stand there. 'How about getting him unsaddled?'

'You don't let up, do you?' she said resignedly, lifting the leathers to get at the girth-strap.

'Where you're concerned, it wouldn't be a good policy.' He put out a hand to push back the lock of blonde hair that had fallen over her cheek, tucking it behind her ear with a touch as light as a feather, adding on a softer note, 'You're too used to having things your way.'

Her pulses were leaping all over the place, her every sense alive to his lean proximity. It was all she could do to keep her voice from reflecting the upheaval that one small gesture had created in her. 'I could say the same about you.'

'*I'm* open to reason.' The hand came to rest on her shoulder, fingers gently moulding the bone. 'Or persuasion.'

Normally that kind of proposition would have evoked a few choice phrases calculated to wither most men where they stood. Right now, Alex was conscious only of the warmth and suppleness in those caressing fingers—of the contained strength. She wanted him to kiss her again, she acknowledged; wanted it badly. She could feel herself tremoring and knew he must feel it too.

'Not something I practise,' she got out against her instincts.

'Try,' he invited. He had moved up behind her, his other hand parting the hair at her nape, breath fluttering over the delicate skin as he brushed his lips across so lightly she could barely feel the contact. 'Who knows what you might achieve.'

He was deliberately taunting her, she realised, well aware of the effect he had on her. She steeled herself against the whisper at the back of her mind that said 'so what?' and jabbed an elbow into his ribs.

Vicious as it was, the dig drew no more than a brief

grunt from him, followed by a laugh that riled her even more.

'If you really want to reckon, you should go for the more vulnerable areas, honey!'

'I'll remember that next time you come near me!' she snapped, without turning as he let her go.

'Forewarned is forearmed,' he mocked. 'Sling the saddle over the rail there. It'll be needed later.'

Alex did as he said only because it gave her time to collect herself, outwardly at least. Inside she was a bundle of conflicting emotions, not least of which was annoyance with herself for the way she had handled the situation. The way to deal with such tactics was to ridicule the perpetrator, not allow him to see her affected by them.

It couldn't be much more than five o'clock even now, the sky only just beginning to turn from grey to palest blue. Having taken the bay back to the corral, Cal brought the harness across to hang it beside the saddle. For the first time Alex noted his shadowed jaw and bed-tousled hair, the jeans and shirt obviously dragged on in a hurry.

'If I woke you passing your door, how come you took so long getting here?' she said.

He shrugged briefly. 'It wasn't so much a noise that woke me. More like a sixth sense. You were already up when I got outside.'

Minus the mockery this time, the grey eyes turned her way again, dwelling for a breath-shortening moment on the curve of her mouth before lifting to meet her hastily veiled gaze. 'We're moving one of the herds this morning if you feel like taking part,' he added.

'Peace offering?' she asked before she could stop herself, regretting it as she saw one dark brow tilt.

'I hadn't thought of it like that, but I've no objection if you want to see it that way. We'll be eating at half-six, leaving at seven. Just remember—'

'To follow orders,' she finished for him with irony. 'Believe me, it's engraved on my heart!'

His eyes followed the hand she pressed to her breast in exaggerated and unthinking emphasis, his smile slow. 'It had better be!'

CHAPTER FIVE

THERE was no sign, on their reaching the house, of either Greg or Margot being up and about as yet. Cal took his things across to their bathroom, leaving the other free for Alex to use.

Wearing another of the chambray shirts she had brought with her, and with her hair done into a thick plait down her back to keep it out of the way, she was ready by six. She had heard Cal go down some minutes before, but there was no sign of him when she got down herself, although noises from the kitchen region in the rear of the house suggested that breakfast was under way.

Several of the hands were already saddling up down at the corrals, she saw from the veranda. In readiness for the off as soon as they'd eaten, she assumed. Cal was there too, a foot propped easily on a lower rail as he conversed with one of the older men. Both Jed and the bay were among those being got ready. Perhaps, Alex thought hopefully, he was planning on letting her ride the latter after all.

'You're up bright and early!' commented Greg, coming to join her at the veranda rail.

'So are you,' she said.

His mouth twisted. '*I* don't have any choice.'

'Are things really so different from what you imagined?' she asked after a moment. 'I mean, you must have realised that a working ranch—'

'I was given the impression that it was run purely as

70

a guest ranch,' he said. 'Oh, not in so many words, maybe, but it was what Margot wanted me to think.'

'Perhaps she was afraid you might lose interest in her if you knew the truth?'

The shrug was defensive. 'It wasn't *just* the ranch. She's a sweet kid.'

Alex winged him a glance, searching the handsome features for some sign of deeper feeling. 'Is that *all* she means to you?'

'I'm not wildly in love with her, if that's what you mean,' he admitted, 'but she isn't losing out on the deal.'

'Yes, she is!' Alex was too angered by the callousness of that bald statement to temper her own words. 'You cheated her, Greg!'

'What would you know about it?' He was angry himself now. 'You haven't spent the last eight years wandering from pillar to post. It's been no picnic, believe me!'

'You could have come back any time you wanted,' she protested. 'I'd have sent you the money myself if you'd given me any inkling you felt like that.'

'Back to what? Even if I'd been able to get a job, I'd have had nowhere to live. That flat of yours doesn't sound big enough to swing a cat in.'

'Mum would have welcomed you with open arms!'

'Sure she would. And *he* would have kicked me straight back out again!'

'His name is James,' Alex returned tautly. 'If you can't say "Dad" at least make that concession. He never did you any harm.'

'You wouldn't know that either.'

It was the bitterness as much as the words themselves that got through to her. She gazed at him in confusion, unable to accept the intimation.

'What exactly are you saying?' she got out. 'I don't remember him ever laying a finger on you—even when you piled the pressure on.'

A muscle jerked just below Greg's cheekbone as his jaw tensed. 'I'd have killed him if he'd tried it, and he knew it! That's why he wanted me out. He gave me the money to join that group. A thousand pounds for a promise to stay out of his life.' He shrugged again at her doubting expression. 'You can believe it or not. I don't suppose he's likely to admit it.'

He wouldn't lie, Alex told herself. Not about something like this. Reconciling the image he presented with the stepfather she knew was difficult, but it explained such a lot she had found even more difficult to understand at the time. She and her mother had been devastated by Greg's sudden decision to up sticks and go running off round the world, while James had shown little emotion at all. If her mother ever found out what he'd done, heaven only knew how she'd react.

'Why didn't you tell me?' she said hollowly.

'Because it wouldn't have helped. You were still in school—with plans to go on to university. I wasn't going to spoil that for you.'

'I never got there anyway. My own fault, of course. I wouldn't listen to anyone who tried telling me how short-sighted I was being.'

'Was he—James—one of them?'

'Not to any extent. I think both he and Mum were as much turned on by the modelling, by the excitement of it all as I was.'

Greg eyed her curiously. 'It can't have been a bad life, though.'

'There are a lot worse ways of earning a living,' she agreed. 'And I haven't been short of jobs, even if they weren't the top ones going. I suppose what it boils down to is that I was never really cut out for the lifestyle.'

The temptation to unload still further was almost overwhelming; she resisted it with difficulty. Greg had problems of his own, without taking hers on board. The sooner she put the whole thing out of mind herself, the better. She made an effort to smile, shaking her head in self-deprecation. 'A sob story, if ever I heard one! Anyway, it's all in the past.'

'You were serious, then, about giving it up?'

'Yes.' She could say that with even more certainty than a couple of days ago. 'I'll probably be taking that sales job I was offered. The money isn't bad, and it will give me time to look round for something else.'

'How about staying on over here?'

Her laugh was short. 'There's hardly much chance of that!'

'There could be if you play your cards right. Cal's ripe for the picking.'

'Not by me,' she retorted, smothering the sudden ache. 'I've no death wish!'

The pause was lengthy. Alex was the first to break it, unable to hold back the question that had preyed on her mind since yesterday.

'Why did you let Margot think you had no family, Greg?'

There was no visible reaction in her brother's face; she had the feeling that he had sensed the query coming.

'It was easier at the time,' he said flatly.

As explanations went it left a lot to be desired, but it was the only one she was going to get, Alex judged. 'So why the change of heart?' she asked.

'I wanted to see you again. Simple as that.' He straightened away from the rail as Margot emerged from the house in obvious haste, expression lightening. 'Whoa, there!'

'You didn't waken me!' she accused plaintively.

'You were sleeping like a baby,' he said, and gave her a lazy smile. 'I thought you might need to catch up.'

She laughed, a faint colour coming and going in her cheeks. 'No more than you. We're moving the herd this morning,' she added to Alex. 'Why don't you come too?'

'Cal already suggested it,' Alex admitted, and received surprised looks from both quarters.

'When?' asked Greg, glancing down to where the Lazy Y boss was still talking then back to her, with sudden speculation in his eyes.

'Oh, a few minutes ago,' she prevaricated hastily, recognising the source of that speculation. 'Are any of the guests lending a hand?'

Margot shook her head. 'Most of them are going hot-air ballooning over the other side of Prescott.'

'I'd better go and saddle-up,' said Greg. 'I'll see to Calico for you, Margot. Know which one you're supposed to be riding?' he asked his sister.

'I'm hoping it will be the bay alongside Jed there,' she said.

'Jingo?' Margot sounded dubious. 'He's a bit of a handful.'

'Alex could handle him.' Greg started down the step. 'See you at breakfast, girls.'

Margot watched him stride away, her pretty little face all too revealing. Alex watched him too, hoping he would continue to play his part as well as he appeared to have done last night. Making love to someone as lovely as Margot could hardly be unpalatable for him, whatever depth of feeling was missing. He should think himself the luckiest man alive!

It was just the four of them at table, the hands being served in a separate dining room off to the rear of the house, and the guests not due across for another hour.

'You'll need more than toast and coffee to see you through the morning,' advised Cal when Alex refused the ham and eggs. He took a plate and served a generous helping of each from the loaded platters, finishing up with a ladle of beans. 'Get that down, or you don't come,' he said, placing it in front of her.

He meant it; she knew him well enough already to be sure of that. Sighing, she set to, surprised to find herself actually enjoying the food once she overcame the initial reluctance.

'Not so difficult, was it?' Cal commented when she finished.

'Must be all the fresh air and exercise I got yesterday that gave me an appetite,' she returned blandly. 'I hope whichever horse I'm riding is up to carrying the extra weight.'

'Alex was fancying Jingo,' Margot put in. 'I told her what a handful he can be.'

Her brother's mouth slanted. 'He's not on his own.'

'Does that mean yes or no?' asked Alex, refusing to rise to the taunt she could see in his eyes.

'A provisional yes,' he said. 'That means you exchange with one of the boys if he starts giving you any trouble.' He pushed back his chair. 'Time we got moving.'

Of the four hands waiting with the horses, only one was younger than his employer. Fair-haired and boldly good-looking, he regarded Alex with an interest that increased by leaps and bounds when she mounted the bay.

'You're the first female ever rode that horse,' he remarked, coming up alongside as they headed out.

'There's a first time for everything,' she returned lightly. 'Have you been with the Lazy Y long?'

'Couple of years. Hear tell you do modelling,' he added. 'Never met a real live model before.'

'I never met a real live cowboy before I came here,' she countered.

His grin was appealing, belying the brazen appraisal of her vital statistics. 'New experience for both of us, then. Maybe we should get together and swap life stories.'

She'd known some fast approaches, thought Alex, struggling between amusement and annoyance, but this beat all. About as subtle as a charging rhinoceros!

He moved his mount on as Cal fell in alongside, joining one of the other hands up front. Alex glanced sideways at the Lazy Y boss, stomach curling, as always, at the impact of that hard-hewn profile.

'Good as gold up to now,' she said flippantly. 'Both of us.'

'Early days yet,' came the dry reply. 'What was Royd after?'

The same thing most men she'd met up to now were after, she could have answered with point—except that she wasn't so sure about Cal's own motives. 'Just passing the time of day,' she said instead.

'From what I saw, the time of day was the last thing on his mind. I want his attention on the job I pay him for, so don't encourage him.'

He moved on before she could respond, leaving her fuming over the intimation that she might even consider it. Royd's type needed no encouragement to start with.

She was still simmering when they reached the herd,

but forgot about it in the excitement of the next half-hour as the animals were rounded up into a reluctant mass. It was frustrating to sit out and watch while the men did all the work, but she had to acknowledge that a greenhorn would only get in the way.

Considering his professed lack of interest in ranch work, Greg was giving a surprisingly good account of himself. He was more against the enforcement than the job itself, Alex concluded.

'I suppose Greg gets to take a turn at supervising guest activities too?' she asked Margot, who was sitting out with her, on a casual note.

'Not as often as he'd like,' the younger girl admitted. She flushed a little. 'I guess I might have put a bit too much emphasis on that side of things when I told him about the Lazy Y. It sounded so much more impressive.'

'I'm sure you didn't need to impress him any more than you already had done.' Not exactly the truth but necessary, Alex told herself firmly. Margot needed to believe that he felt as much for her as she did for him if they were to have any chance at all. 'He's obviously crazy about you,' she added, with all the conviction she could muster. 'If he isn't too demonstrative about it, that's just the way English men are.'

Margot gave a secretive little smile. 'I've heard that said before, but it isn't true. Not all the time anyway.' She stood up in the stirrups to wave a hand in acknowledgement of her brother's signal. 'They're ready to start moving them out.'

It was a leisurely progress. So far as Alex was concerned, there could be few things more pleasurable than ambling along in the sun with the animal scents mingling in her nostrils, the sounds filling her ears. They were moving on grass, so there wasn't even any dust to contend with, the mountains etched clear and sharp against a sky lightly ribbed with high cirrus cloud. Pure unadulterated heaven!

Cal was riding rearguard, urging on any would-be grazers. He and Jed made the perfect team, man and horse in both physical and intuitive harmony. Furious though that masculine assertion might make her at times, she could hardly deny being drawn to him. Too much so, she thought wryly, considering the temporary nature of her time here. It was going to be hard enough leaving this dream-world of hers at all, without making it even worse by falling for the man.

'You're doing real well,' Royd congratulated her, dropping back alongside. 'Got a mind of his own that horse, but he sure ain't having it all his own way with you! Guess you're tougher than you look,' he added with a grin. 'Maybe you—'

Royd broke off as a steer suddenly bolted out from the general herd, some distance ahead where he should have been riding, urging his horse into immediate pursuit of the runaway. Alex felt Jingo tense beneath her when a second steer made a break right in front of them, and was unable to hold him, hanging on by the skin of her teeth as he twisted and turned with incredible speed and agility to bring the escapee back into line.

'Good going!' called Royd. 'Keep it up, gal!'

Clamping her hat more firmly on her head, Alex grinned back at him, her former antipathy forgotten in the thrill of the moment. 'I sure will!'

Margot came up on her offside, pulling the pinto she was riding sharply out of the way as Jingo aimed a sudden vicious nip at the smaller animal.

'Cal says you're to drop back,' she shouted above the general clamour.

'Why?' Alex demanded, having trouble controlling the bay at all now, but determined not to give in. 'I'm okay here!'

'You'd better do it, or he'll come and make you,' her sister-in-law advised.

Let him try! was Alex's first thought; Stop playing the recalcitrant heroine, her second, as common sense took over. She'd been closer than she'd ever been to coming off back there and Cal would know it. He wouldn't risk it happening again.

Jingo fought her when she started to turn him, rearing like a circus pony to paw the air in protest at the pressure on his mouth. Next moment he was streaking away from the herd in a headstrong gallop she stood no chance of pulling him out from.

How far they'd gone before Jed's head came into view on the periphery of her vision Alex couldn't have said. It seemed miles. Her arms felt like lead from the strain of hauling back on the reins—for what good it was doing—her thigh muscles locked. Jingo showed no sign of tiring. Even the considerable rise they'd just topped had had little effect.

Bent forward in the saddle to cut down wind resistance, mouth grimly set, Cal urged the grey forward inch by inch until the two horses were running neck to neck, reaching with one hand to seize the bay's rein close up by the bit then applying brakes to his own mount.

It took the combined strength of both man and horse to slow the runaway enough for Alex herself to regain some control. Even then, it was several more minutes before he came to a full halt, standing with heaving, sweat-frothed flanks, the fury finally run.

Alex slid to the ground, limbs like jelly, steeling herself to meet Cal's eyes as he dismounted.

'That wasn't deliberate,' she said huskily. 'I couldn't hold him. Honestly.'

'I could see that,' he responded tautly. 'My fault for letting you ride the damned animal in the first place! If you'd taken a spill at that speed—' He broke off, shaking his head. 'That's it. He goes out to grass!'

'You can't!' she protested. 'He's too good a cow-pony—you said it yourself. I'll leave him alone from now on, promise.' She gave a shaky laugh. 'I'm beginning to realise my limitations!'

'Something, I suppose.' He looked down at her upturned face in narrowed appraisal. 'Feeling okay?'

She was feeling quivery, but not from delayed shock. Cal was too close for comfort—his mouth on a level with her eyes, the scent of him in her nostrils, the whole lean, hard length of him a spur to her senses. More man than she had ever met before, and would probably ever meet again—and she wanted him, desperately, the heat spreading from some central core throughout her whole body as she gazed at him, stirring emotions she could control no better than she had controlled the bay.

He knew, of course. Judging from the expression that sprang to sudden life in the grey eyes, he was by no means unresponsive either. Unlike the morning, he didn't tease, just pulled her to him and kissed her, lips demanding, forceful, almost angry at first; then softening as she responded, his tongue a subtle explorer, tasting the inner sweetness, his hands moving down her back to bring her to him, making her aware of his arousal.

The blood hammering in her ears, Alex was past thinking about anything beyond this moment. It was like being doused in cold water when he abruptly released her.

'We'd better get back to the herd before someone

comes looking for us,' he said briefly. 'You ride Jed. I'll take Jingo.'

Totally deflated, Alex could conjure no protest as he hoisted her into the grey's saddle. While he might return the desire, he obviously had no intention of fulfilling it. All she'd succeeded in doing was cheapening herself, she thought hollowly. He probably took it that she gave the same come-on to every man she met.

The stallion was none too enthusiastic, at first, about having a stranger on his back, but a word from Cal calmed him down. Jingo gave no trouble at all. Moving at a far slower speed than before, and allowing for the distance the herd would have travelled between times, it took them close on fifteen minutes to reach it.

Hat pulled down over his eyes to shade them from the sun, body easy in the saddle, Cal looked untouched by anything that had happened back there. But then, so far as he was concerned, nothing had, Alex reflected numbly. She was the one suffering rejection.

Margot cantered up as they fell in at the rear, concern written large on her face.

'Are you okay?' she asked.

'Fine,' Alex assured her, lying through her teeth. She conjured a grin in support of her claim, aware of Cal's proximity. 'Hurt pride, that's all!'

The rest of the drive was relatively uneventful. With the herd contentedly grazing the new pasture, the whole party headed back to the ranch. Jed had started playing up a little over the final stretch, so Cal had ordered a three-way swap with one of the hands, which meant Alex was now riding yet another different horse. At this rate, she thought, she would soon have gone through the whole remuda!

The hot-air ballooning party was back in time for

lunch too. Considering the breakfast she had eaten, and the emotional turmoil she was still suffering, Alex was amazed to find herself with an appetite at all, much less a ravenous one. She did full justice to a large plate of cold-cuts and salad, followed by apple pie and cream.

'You'll need plenty of room for tonight,' advised Margot over coffee on the veranda. 'Buck's cookouts are legend! It's a weekly get-together for everybody. Sing-alongs round the camp-fire and all that. The married men bring their wives and kids over, the others bring girlfriends—those who've got them. The way Royd was hanging round you this morning, he already transferred *his* interests,' she added slyly.

Cal was in earshot, though apparently absorbed in discussion with a couple of the male guests. Alex smiled and shrugged. 'Not my type.'

'What type *do* you go for?'

'Tall, dark and devastating' was the phrase that sprang to mind. 'Generous, gentle and trustworthy,' she said, and saw Cal's mouth take on a definite slant.

'Hooey!' came the derisive retort from his sister. 'You'd be bored out of your mind!'

Chance would be a fine thing, Alex reflected drily, but she knew her sister-in-law was right. What she needed was a man capable of making her feel the way Cal made her feel, and no gentle soul was going to do that.

He disappeared indoors shortly after, while Greg went off to see to some unspecified job.

Led by one of the wranglers, a small party of guests went out riding for the afternoon, while others elected to toss horseshoes or practise archery. There was no rigid routine at the Lazy Y; everyone did whatever they felt like doing. Some, it seemed, didn't bother with the extraneous entertainments at all. Alex could understand that.

Compared with ranch life itself, hot-air ballooning and such held little appeal for her either.

At five, she went up with Margot to get a shower and change for the evening. The dress code was much the same as usual, she had gathered. One or two of the women might turn up in skirts and blouses, or even a dress, but the majority would stick to jeans and shirt, with a sweater for later on when it got cool.

After so many years of dressing for the job, it made a restful change not to have to think about what to wear. She made one concession by tying a jaunty red neckerchief at the open throat of her blue and white checked shirt, leaving her hair hanging free to her shoulders. Despite the shading of her hat brim, her face was already touched by the sun, she noted.

Her eyes lacked their customary sparkle; she made an effort to renew it. So she'd allowed her emotions to get a little out of hand earlier. That didn't mean she had to go around with a face like a wet weekend! The physical side apart, Cal meant no more to her than she did to him.

The big iron barbecue grills at the back of the house were already lit when she got outside. Trestle tables set out alongside were groaning beneath the weight of food, with more appearing by the minute. People were already starting to arrive, the ranch guests strolling across from their cabins, the bachelor hands from the bunk house, others coming in via various means of transport. The delicious smell of chargrilled steak filled the air.

Six feet two of pure masculinity in narrow black Levi's and matching shirt, a blue neckerchief at his throat, Cal was talking with a large family group that had just arrived. He beckoned her over, nothing untoward in his manner as he introduced her around. Alex did her best to project the same easy attitude, but it was purely surface.

Three days to get to this stage, she thought wryly, unable to sustain the pretence. She had fallen, and fallen hard; why not admit it? She wasn't the first to go overboard for the man. So far, Diane had failed to put in an appearance. Not that she meant anything vital to him either, from what he had said yesterday, but that could change in time. As a rancher's daughter she was eminently suitable to become a rancher's wife.

A cry of 'Food's up!' had most people surging in the direction of the grills. Alex went with them, unwilling to have Cal think she might be waiting for him to take her over.

'On your own?' asked Royd, appearing at her elbow as she joined the line-up. 'Now there's a lucky break! How about I bag a couple of plates while you find somewhere to sit and eat?'

'Fine,' she agreed, unable to come up with any adequate reason why not on the spur of the moment. 'Just a piece of chicken and a baked potato will do me, though. I've eaten too much already.'

'Last thing you need to worry about is your figure,' he said, giving it an admiring once-over. 'Couldn't be better!'

Her figure was the last thing on her mind, but she let it pass. An open fire had been lit some distance from the barbecue grills, with logs drawn into a wide circle about it. Ready for the promised sing-along later, she assumed, although several people had elected to take seats there already rather than at the trestle tables.

Voices mingled, interspersed with laughter from various quarters. Children ran about happily, watched over by everyone. These people were so obviously content with their lives, Alex reflected, not a little enviously. She would give just about anything to become a member of such a community.

'What are you doing over here?' asked Cal, jerking her out of her thoughts. 'Don't you want anything to eat?'

'Someone's fetching me something,' she said, hoping he couldn't hear the blood racing round her veins. 'I'm supposed to be finding a seat.'

His eyes narrowed a little. 'Royd, by any chance?'

'Well, yes, as a matter of fact. He offered. I—'

'You just couldn't turn him down!' The tone was sardonic.

Alex felt her whole body tauten like a bow-string. 'Not without giving the impression that a mere ranchhand wasn't good enough to eat with, no. I always thought all Americans were equal.'

'And all men fair game?'

She drew in a sharp breath. 'I'm eating with him, that's all!'

'He'll be looking for more than that.'

Alex made every effort to control her fast rising temper. 'Well, he won't be getting it. Contrary to what you might think, I'm no easy lay!'

There was a hint of cruelty in the curl of his lip. 'You're saying I misread what you were offering *me* this afternoon?'

Her head jerked as if he'd hit her, the colour coming and going in her face. Her voice sounded thick. 'The way you mean it, yes.'

'How many ways are there? I may be from the backwoods,' he added with irony, 'but the language is much the same.'

'In that case,' she got out, 'I'm surprised you didn't take advantage.'

'Wrong time, wrong place. Typical of a woman!'

The anger flooding her was a saving grace. 'I'm sure you'd know!'

Her raised voice drew curious glances from those in the vicinity. She bit her lip, wondering how she could have imagined herself even fractionally in love with this man. Looking at him now, so unyielding in his masculine arrogance, she felt closer to hatred. He'd denigrated what to her had been a great deal more than just basic lust.

'Cool it,' Cal advised as she opened her mouth to deliver another, if quieter, broadside. 'Folks will think we're having a lovers' tiff!'

The spark that leapt in her eyes was matched by the fury in her heart, driving out everything but the urge to hit back. She gave a sudden laugh, reaching up with both hands to draw his head down to hers and plant a lingering kiss on his lips. 'Sorry, darling!' she said, loud enough for the same people to hear. 'I don't know what I was thinking of!'

The grey eyes had a spark of their own when she let go of him, his smile a dangerous edge. 'That's all right, honey,' he responded. 'I'll make allowances—this time.'

There was a spurt of laughter from the nearby group. 'Way to go, man!' somebody said.

Cal gave a brief grin, sliding a hard arm about Alex's shoulders. 'Let's go find some food.'

He headed for the house, not the barbecue grills, keeping her pinioned at his side. Judging from the line of his mouth, he had every intention of extracting payment for that little piece of play-acting, Alex concluded. Not that *she* had any intention of paying—in any shape or form!

'Far enough,' she said between her teeth. 'Just get your hands off me, Cal!'

'When I'm good and ready,' he returned unequivocally, slicing a smile at a couple just passing. 'You want folk to think we're getting it together, you got it!'

'All this because one of your men dared to trespass on your preserves?' she taunted, too enraged to consider any consequences. 'Or what you *thought* were your preserves! And there I was, thinking droit de seigneur only applied to *feudal* lords!'

'It applied to brides on their wedding night, which hardly fits the bill either,' came the maddeningly accurate reply. 'Smile, honey. We're under surveillance.'

Sitting with Greg and some other people on the veranda, Margot looked at the two of them with open approval as they came up the step together.

'Come and join us?' she invited. 'We were just debating whether to go for food now or wait till the rush subsides.'

'Best to wait,' Cal advised, coming to halt at the table. 'There's plenty to go round.'

'There always is,' claimed a red-headed young woman who looked to be with one of the wranglers. 'You put on a real good spread, Cal.'

'Generous to a fault,' Alex agreed smoothly, seizing her chance. 'Personally, I could eat a horse right now, if anybody feels like keeping me company?'

'I'll come,' said the redhead, getting up. 'I didn't eat all day so I could stuff myself tonight!'

'I guess we'd better all go before she clears the lot,' grinned her boyfriend. 'You never saw anybody can put it away like this one!'

Anticipating opposition from Cal, Alex was almost

disappointed when he allowed her to slide out from under his arm without protest.

'I'll hang fire,' he said easily. 'Time enough yet.'

Not if she had anything to do with it! she thought forcefully, beating a retreat. She'd show the domineering swine what his opinions were worth!

CHAPTER SIX

ROYD was looking round for her, a couple of loaded plates in his hands.

'I was beginning to think you'd ditched me,' he said. 'You found somewhere to sit?'

Ignoring Margot's questioning glance, Alex nodded in the direction of the fire. 'The logs aren't occupied.'

'Suits me,' he agreed readily. 'I've been waiting to get you on your own all day.'

For what good it was going to do him, she reflected. She had met too many of Royd's type during the last few years; their egos needed the occasional deflation. Cal's could do with it too. She hoped he was watching right now!

Surprisingly, Royd turned out to be not bad company when he forgot the Don Juan routine, making her laugh with his comments on life in the bunk house. He'd worked ranches since leaving school, he said. There wasn't a lot else in these parts. His family lived over Burlington way. Too far to come in every day like some.

Led by one of the wranglers on guitar, the sing-along went with a swing. Alex even recognised a tune or two herself. Royd was frankly bored by it all, saying it was only put on for the guests, but everyone else seemed to enjoy it—the children in particular. There was an occasional glimpse of Cal in the glow of the firelight but he made no attempt to come near.

The family groups started drifting away around nine-thirty. By half-past ten most of the rest had gone too, but some stayed on to help clear the debris.

The camaraderie among these people was enviable in itself, thought Alex, leaving a disgruntled Royd to his own devices while she carried a stack of plates through to the kitchen. So totally unlike the self-seeking society she was accustomed to.

Born here, she would never have met a man like Morgan Baxter—never have had to suffer the shame of having her name linked, even fleetingly, with such a man. No one—Greg included—would be likely to consider her entirely blameless if they ever got to hear the story. Not that they were likely to hear it, thank heaven!

Royd was no longer around when she got outside again. Apparently quicker to take a hint than she had given him credit for, she thought, relieved not to be faced with any problems from that quarter. Spending the evening with him just to cock a snook at Cal had hardly been an adult gesture to start with.

With the last of the visiting vehicles departed, and the guests returned to their cabins, Margot announced her intention of following Greg, who had already gone up to bed.

'I don't know where Cal got to,' she said. 'Last I saw of him was half an hour ago or more.'

'Perhaps he was tired,' Alex suggested. 'It's been a long day.'

'For all of us,' Margot agreed. She hesitated before saying diffidently, 'Do you really prefer Royd's company?'

Alex gave a wry little smile and a shrug. 'It wasn't like that.'

'You mean you were trying to make Cal jealous?'

'More a retaliation.'

Hazel eyes cleared. 'Oh, I see! He'd told you to stay away from Royd, and you objected to being told. Not very clever on his part.'

'Even less on mine,' Alex conceded.

'Oh, well, it will sort itself out.' Margot sounded cheerfully confident. 'Are you coming up?'

Alex shook her head. 'I think I'll sit out here on the veranda for a while first, and just enjoy the peace.'

'Well, don't fall asleep out here, or you'll finish up chilled through in the early hours. Breakfast at seven-thirty for everybody in the morning, by the way, so we can get into town good and early.'

'I'll be there,' Alex promised. 'Night, Margot.'

Alone and in silence, but for the general night sounds, she stood hugging an upright post as she looked out on the moonlit landscape, going over the day's events in her mind's eye.

What she had felt when Cal kissed her this morning she was still feeling now—a deep-down ache that instinct told her would only be pacified one way. She had read so many accounts, both fictional and non-fictional, of what sexual arousal should feel like but she'd never experienced it with any real intensity until today.

Just one time, more than a year ago, she had gone to bed with a man she had believed was someone special, but no bells had rung or earth moved. With Cal it would be different; the way she reacted to his kisses alone was proof of that. Only after tonight it was doubtful if she'd have the chance to find out.

'Waiting for someone?' came the sardonic query from the doorway behind her, and she tensed involuntarily, unable to stifle the sharp exclamation as her grasp shifted and something stabbed into her palm.

'Not you!' she snapped back, driven by the sudden stinging pain.

The fingers fastening on her shoulder to jerk her round were hard enough to bruise. Lean features set, eyes glittering, he looked ready to do something drastic to her. 'Don't—' he began, and immediately broke off, expression altering as he saw the hand she was clutching to her chest. 'What did you do?'

Alex shook her head, already regretting the brusqueness. 'It's nothing. Just stings a bit, that's all.'

Cal let go of her shoulder to take the hand instead, straightening out her fingers with a gentleness that unnerved her even more than the violence had done. The long, thin splinter had run under her skin the whole length of her palm's outer edge. He gave vent to a low, sympathetic whistle.

'That must be hurting like hell! Nothing I can do about it here. Come on inside.'

He kept his hand lightly under her elbow for support on the way. Hardly necessary, but a comfort just the same, Alex admitted, clenching her teeth against the throbbing pain. She was a jelly baby when it came to injuries of this nature, minor though it might be. Just the thought of drawing the darn thing out again was enough to cause palpitations.

Cal sat her down in the big, empty living-room and went to fetch the first-aid box. He was also carrying a small bowl of hot water and a bottle of disinfectant when he returned. Alex watched in trepidation as he opened the well-stocked box to extract a pair of tweezers.

'Lucky there's an end still showing,' he said. 'It should come out in one piece.' He grasped her wrist to hold the hand still, not looking at her directly. 'Close your eyes if it helps.'

It was over in seconds, but they were some of the longest seconds of her life. She drew in a trembling breath of sheer relief as the blood-soaked splinter slid clear. The disinfectant stung too, but she could stomach that. Cal applied a coating of antiseptic cream as an extra precaution against infection from the treated wood.

'It should be okay,' he said, peeling a plaster to fit over the wound. 'We'll keep an eye on it all the same. I'll have that post sanded down before there's any further damage done.'

He was still down on one knee before her, head bent to his task. It took everything Alex had to stop herself from reaching out her free hand to touch the dark hair. She could imagine the feel of that springing density beneath her fingers, as soft as the rest of him was hard.

Sensing her regard, he looked up, his eyes starting a burn of their own as he registered the desire she was unable to banish from hers. He pulled her up along with him as he got to his feet, sliding both hands into the thickness of her hair to tilt her head, pressuring open her lips with a long, slow seeking that reached each and every part of her.

His hands slid down her back to bring her closer, making her aware of every hard male contour. She was lost in a world of sensation, mind blanked of everything but the growing need. She moved instinctively against him, feeling his response and wanting more of him—wanting him to know more of her.

The fingers unbuttoning her shirt were dextrous, the hand he slid inside to seek the contour of her breast a revelation in its sensitivity. Somehow, he managed to snap open the clip at her back with his free hand, baring both breasts to his exploration. Alex felt the breath catch in her throat as he lowered his head to follow the same path with his lips and tongue, back arching to the exquisite sensation.

Three days, three weeks, three months—what did it matter how long or short a time it had taken to get here? It was the only place she wanted to be.

She went willingly when he drew her down onto a nearby sofa, making no protest when he slid her shirt off altogether along with her brassière. Her skin looked like alabaster against the brown of his hands. Strong hands, yet gentle too, the brush of a thumb over her tingling, aching nipple almost too much so.

Fingers trembling a little, she opened his shirt, pressing her lips to the smooth, damp skin beneath and inhaling the musky male scent. Her tongue came out to touch and taste, drawing a guttural sound from his lips as she traced a spiralling line through the coating of dark hair.

'You'd better not be playing games this time,' he said thickly.

'I'm not.' She lifted her head to look into his eyes, too far over the top to be coy about it. 'I want you, Cal!'

The smile was slow. 'Maybe as well, considering.' He reached for the shirt he had recently taken from her. 'Better put that on, just in case we run into anyone.'

'Going where?' she asked blankly, and saw one dark brow lift.

'Where would you think?'

Alex had been concerned only with the here and now—carried along on the crest of a wave she had been both unable and unwilling to resist. The thought of breaking off in order to go upstairs to a bedroom was somehow deflating.

'I grew out of sofas and the back seat of cars a long time ago,' he said softly, watching the flicker of expression across her face. 'I'd have thought you had too. Apart from which, I don't have anything with me right now.'

He meant protection, of course. Sensible of him, Alex supposed, but soul-destroying in its implication. Telling him just how rare an event this was for her would be a waste of time. His opinion of her kind had been formed before she even got here. A man didn't have to respect a woman in order to contemplate having her; hadn't she learned that yet?

She drew on the shirt and fastened the buttons without looking at him, all desire flown. 'I've changed my mind,' she said flatly. 'Woman's prerogative and all that.'

It was a moment or two before he answered. When he did speak it was in measured tones all the more dangerous for their lack of force. 'And what makes you think I'll be prepared to accept it?'

Alex forced herself to meet the grey eyes, quailing inwardly at the steely glint but maintaining a surface control. 'Because whatever else you might be, I doubt if you'd stoop to rape.'

His lip curled. 'And you reckon that's what I'd have to do?'

'I don't reckon, I know!' she snapped back, unable to stem the anger any longer. 'We're not all bimbos!'

There was no softening of expression in his eyes. 'You'll be telling me next that you're still a virgin.'

'Nearer to it than you are, for certain!' she flashed. 'Different for a man, of course!'

His smile lacked humour. 'Every time.'

The fight went out of her suddenly. 'Think what you like,' she said tonelessly. 'I'm going to bed.'

Face devoid of emotion, Cal made no attempt to stop

her as she got unsteadily to her feet. Only as she started to move away did he speak.

'Forgotten something?'

He was dangling the flimsy lace brassière from a finger when she turned back to look at him. Alex took it with what dignity she could muster, feeling the heat rising under her skin. For a fleeting moment something akin to doubt flickered his steely eyes, then he shook his head as if in dismissal of whatever thought had crossed his mind.

'Don't get any dirt in that hand,' he said.

Alex made no answer, just turned on her heel and left him sitting there, the pain in her hand nothing compared to the tightness in her chest.

She'd been a fool to look for anything better than what she had got from him. So far as Cal was concerned, she fitted the universal media profile of her profession to a T. Considering the way she had behaved since getting here—and in particular tonight—she could hardly blame him too much for that.

The best thing she could do was go home, she thought hollowly, mounting the stairs. She'd made a complete mess of things here. She would check on flight availability tomorrow in town; there was a travel agent on Main Street.

Neither Greg nor Cal put in an appearance at breakfast. 'Things to see to,' said Margot when asked where the boss was by the woman who made a point of seating herself close by him whenever possible. He would be riding in the rodeo, she confirmed, though not until the afternoon. So, she added, to Alex's surprise, would Greg be too.

With most of the female guests eager to do some last-minute shopping, they were in town by nine-thirty. Alex gave Margot the slip in order to call on the travel agent, hardly knowing whether to be dismayed or relieved on finding that the soonest she could hope to get on a flight was Thursday of the following week. She made a provisional booking and asked to be advised of any cancellations, emerging from the agency in time to spot Margot going into the department store where she had bought her hat.

'I've been looking everywhere for you!' the younger girl exclaimed when she caught up with her. 'Where did you get to?'

'I took a wrong turning,' Alex said vaguely, hoping she wouldn't be asked how she could possibly have done that in a town with so relatively few turnings at all. 'I wouldn't mind getting some boots while we're in here,' she added, in order to change the subject, remembering too late that she was hardly going to have much use for them any more. They would serve as a souvenir along with her hat, she thought resignedly.

'What are you planning to wear tonight?' asked her sister-in-law, pausing to finger through some colourful skirts on the way out of the store. 'You'd look wonderful in one of these, especially with one of those off-the-shoulder blouses over there.'

Alex eyed her questioningly. 'Tonight?'

'The dance. We'll all be going—guests included. It's the high spot of the week.' She unhooked a full swirling cotton in mingled blues, holding it up to Alex's waist. 'Try it on, why don't you? And the blouse.'

'I don't really think—' Alex began, then broke off, giving a smiling little shrug. 'Okay, I'll try it, but it isn't really my style.'

Her style or not, she had to admit that she rather liked

the effect when she saw herself in the dressing-room mirror, shoulders bared by the beautifully embroidered white drawstring blouse, waist tightly cinched above slenderly curved hips. The white sandals she had packed as a last-minute addition would be suitable for dancing in. If she never wore it again, at least she would look right for the night.

Margot was delighted with the decision. 'You'll have steam coming out of all the men's ears when you turn up in that outfit!' she announced gleefully.

Not Cal's, Alex thought wryly. He'd done all the steaming he was going to do last night.

They joined the rest of the party for lunch at one of the town diners before going on to claim ready-booked seats in the packed stadium for the afternoon rodeo contests. Cal and Greg would be behind the scenes with the other competitors by now, Alex assumed, viewing the holding pens on the far side of the arena. Greg was down for the calf-roping, which called for a degree of expertise she wouldn't have thought him capable of as yet.

Event followed event, with scarcely a pause in between. For sheer excitement there was little to beat the sight of man and beast battling for supremacy, Alex conceded, roaring her approval along with hundreds of other spectators as the whistle signalled time-up for a successful competitor. She had had a saddle horn to cling to when Jingo had played up; these real bronco riders were allowed no more than a one-handed grasp of a rein. Staying put for the mandatory eight seconds called for superb balance as well as skill.

'I'd better go get Judy ready for the barrel race,' said Margot, glancing at the programme. 'Did you want to stay here in the stands, or would you rather come on out back where the real action is?'

'I guess I'll go for the action,' Alex drawled, grinning at the pained expression. 'Guess I need some more work on the accent, huh?'

'You're not kidding!' returned the younger girl. Descending the steps at the rear of the stand, she added impulsively, 'I wish you could be here for good, Alex.'

She wasn't alone in that, Alex could have told her, but saw little point. 'I could hardly do what I do for a living in Prescott,' she said instead.

'You could marry Cal,' came the ready answer. 'You'd be terrific together!'

Alex summoned a laugh, aware of the brittleness in the sound. 'Oh, the perfect couple!'

'I'm serious. There's never been anybody strong-minded enough to stand up to him the way you do.'

'That's hardly a basis for marriage.'

'It's not just that. He's attracted to you. I know he is! I'm pretty sure you feel the same way about him too,' she added with a sly sidewards glance.

'It's possible to find someone physically attractive without falling for them hook, line and sinker,' Alex returned lightly. 'Cal's as far from my ideal as I am from his, so you're wasting your time trying to matchmake.'

'It's my time.' Margot sounded undeterred. She looked round as somebody hailed her from one of the pens they were passing, her smile widening on sight of the young man perched astride the upper rail.

'Hi, Randy! Are you bulldogging today?'

'I'm in the next set,' he confirmed. He swung a leg over and climbed down, wiping his hands on the seat of trousers even dustier. 'Greg not with you today?'

'He's with Cal and the boys,' she said. 'This is his sister, out from England on vacation. Meet Randy Colton, Alex.'

For no reason she could have explained, Alex had a sudden notion that this was the man Cal would have preferred Margot to marry. Greg came out the winner in sheer good looks, she supposed, but he lacked the strength of character she could see in the face before her now. Unfortunately, character didn't hold quite the same appeal. Not to someone Margot's age.

'Good to meet you,' he said. 'Staying long?'

'As long as we can keep her here,' declared Margot before she could reply. 'We'd better get moving. I'm in the barrel race. See you at the dance tonight.'

'He seems nice,' Alex ventured as they moved on along the row.

'Randy? Oh, sure. One of the nicest guys I know!' Margot gave her a swift glance. 'Not your type at all.' She grinned and shook her head as Alex raised her eyebrows. 'You know what I mean. You need somebody more forceful.'

'Like your brother?'

'Like my brother,' she agreed imperturbably. 'I'm going to keep on working at it, whatever you say!'

She would receive short shrift from Cal if she tried her matchmaking techniques on him, Alex reflected. After last night's fiasco it was doubtful if he had any interest left in her at all.

They found the Lazy Y contingent preparing for their own up-and-coming events.

'Just something I found I could do pretty good,' said Greg with a shrug, when Alex remarked on his entry.

Cal was busy fastening buckskin chaps over his jeans. She nerved herself to meet his eyes when he looked up, resolved to give no hint of how she was really feeling.

'I hear you're down for the bareback ride?'

'I'm hoping to stay *up* for it,' he answered drily. He

ran a lingering glance over her, taking in the thrust of her breasts beneath the tan silk shirt, the fit of the white jeans about her hips, the shining, finely tooled leather boots. 'You look ready for the camera!'

'I thought a bit more effort was called for today,' she said. 'I'll be going even further tonight.' She felt her colour rise as he lifted an ironic brow, inwardly cursing the unfortunate choice of words. 'For the dance,' she added, and could have bitten her tongue off again as his lips slanted to match.

'You'll be belle of the evening if you turn up in a sack, honey!'

Close enough to have heard the exchange, Royd gave her a sour look, muttering something under his breath as he turned away. There went yet another disillusioned man, Alex thought wryly.

'You're up next, Cal,' someone outside her line of vision called.

He waved a hand in response, moving across immediately to mount the rails of the nearby pen already containing a protesting mustang, dark head glinting with health and vitality in the sunlight. For a second or two he perched astride, judging his moment, then dropped down onto the threshing bare back, taking a firm hold on the single length of rope attached to the animal's halter before signalling readiness to the man operating the gate.

Alex felt her stomach lurch as the enraged bronco erupted into the open, nerve and sinew jerking in sympathy with every stiff-legged, body-slamming impact. The vital eight seconds seemed like a lifetime, but Cal was still there when the whistle went, and looking little the worse for wear.

'Will he have to ride again?' she asked one of the older hands standing nearby.

The wrangler shook his head. 'He doesn't compete for the prize money.'

'Then why do it at all?'

'Needs the challenge, I guess.' He gave her a shrewd glance. 'Reckon you're a bit of a risk-taker yourself.'

'"Foolhardy" might be closer to the mark,' she said wryly, 'but I'm learning.'

Greg put up a fair show in the calf-roping contest, finishing joint seventh, with Royd coming third. The barrel race was won by Diane, Margot trailing way back in fifth place.

'Guess I'm just not aggressive enough,' she said cheerfully when Alex commiserated with her. 'Diane would rather break her neck than not win!'

Her brother gave her an admonishing look. 'Diane won because she rode a better race than anyone else.'

'I'll bet Alex could have beaten her,' Margot returned promptly.

'Hardly,' Alex disclaimed before Cal could answer, wishing her sister-in-law would cut it out. 'How many more events are there?'

'Quite a number,' he said, 'but we'll not be seeing them. We've an early supper scheduled. Bill went to get everybody together.'

'You'll definitely be coming back with us to the dance?' asked Margot.

'Providing nothing crops up to stop me.' He regarded her quizzically. 'Why?'

The shrug was over-casual. 'No special reason.' She slid a hand through Greg's arm. 'Let's go help get them loaded.'

Alex would have preferred to walk with them, but

Margot was obviously intent on leaving her in Cal's company. She was pretty sure that he knew what his sister had in mind, too. Subtlety was hardly the latter's strong point.

'How's the hand?' he asked as they moved down the rear of the pens in the wake of the other two.

'Fine,' she said dismissively, wanting no reminder of last night's fiasco. 'Is the dance a regular event?'

'Most summer Saturdays,' Cal confirmed. 'Not just square dancing. The younger element wouldn't stand for it.'

'You talk as if you've one foot in the grave yourself,' she said, and received an ironic glance.

'I've no interest in teenage pursuits, for sure.'

'I suppose being landed with total responsibility for both the ranch and Margot at the age when most young men are still out sowing their wild oats must have been a sobering experience,' she continued, turning a deaf ear to the innuendo.

'I guess I'd already done all the sowing I was going to do by then.' He lifted a hand in greeting to an older man conversing with a small group by one of the pens. 'Joss.'

Diane appeared suddenly round the corner of the pen, amber eyes lighting up on sight of him. 'I thought I heard your voice!' she said. 'I was about to come looking for you.' The glance she flicked in Alex's direction was as cursory as her nod. 'Hi.'

'Nice to see you again too,' Alex responded levelly, not about to be so easily dismissed. 'Congratulations on your win, by the way.'

'Thanks, but it's no big deal. I win it every year.' She hadn't taken her eyes off Cal, her smile warm and intimate. 'You'll be at the dance tonight?'

'Probably,' he said. 'Save me one, anyway.'

She would so obviously save them all for him if asked, thought Alex as they moved on. From what he had said the other day Diane was as far from getting him to the altar as she was herself, but he must have given her some reason to keep on trying.

'It must be a real boost to your ego having someone like Diane chasing after you,' she remarked, with a cutting edge she couldn't resist. 'You don't even try to get the message across.'

'You just concentrate on getting the message across to Royd,' came the level response. 'I don't want to see him anywhere near you tonight.'

Judging from the way he'd avoided so much as passing the time of day with her this afternoon there wasn't much danger of it, Alex thought, but saw no reason to say it.

'You could always warn him off yourself,' she parried. 'His job has to be worth more to him than a passing fancy.'

'I'm warning *you*!' His voice had gained a rougher edge. 'You've played your last game!'

They were within both sight and hearing of the Lazy Y group being ushered into the two waiting minibuses. Alex bit back the sharp retort, donning a smile for the benefit of anyone looking. What difference did it make? This time next week it would all be behind her.

CHAPTER SEVEN

SUPPER was a lively meal, with the rodeo the main topic of conversation. Apart from one of the older couples, who professed themselves too weary to bother, everyone was planning on returning to town for the evening's entertainment.

'I'm going to be real sorry to leave tomorrow,' declared the middle-aged but not unattractive woman who had asked after the Lazy Y boss that morning. 'If you weren't all booked up next week, Cal, I might have stayed on myself.'

'Well, he is, so you can't,' said her husband drily, obviously not unaware of what the main attraction was. 'Anyway, you were complaining about being saddle-sore only this morning!'

'A week's enough for most,' Cal said easily. 'We get very few staying longer.'

'Apart from Alex.' The older woman eyed her with curiosity mingled with not a little envy. 'Don't you have contracts to fulfil?'

Alex shook her head. 'I work freelance for the most part. It's less restricting.'

'You must be missing out on jobs while you're over here, though.'

'Doesn't matter, does it, seeing you're giving it all up anyway?' said Greg.

'You are?' Margot was all eagerness, vivacious little face alight, mind one-track for the moment.

'When did you make *that* decision?' asked Cal levelly.

Mentally cursing her brother for dropping it out the way he had, Alex lifted her shoulders. 'Greg's jumping the gun. I'm only thinking about it.'

'But why would you want to give it up at all?' asked one of the other women. 'You're so young. You must have years ahead of you!'

'Better to get out at the top than on the way down, maybe?' suggested her partner.

'I was never at the top to start with,' Alex denied, 'but it's still a good maxim. The competition gets fiercer by the year.'

Cal viewed her with an unreadable expression. 'So what do you have in mind as a substitute?'

She made herself meet the grey gaze, hating him for his power to stir her still. 'Nothing concrete. As I said, I'm only thinking about it so far.'

'I guess you'll come up with something.' He glanced at his watch and added decisively, 'We'd better get a move on if we're going to be there for the start. Latecomers don't get a table to sit at between times.'

Alex couldn't see that worrying him any, but the guests' comfort had to be taken into account—especially on their last night. The new intake wasn't due in until Monday, which meant that tomorrow night it would be just the four of them for supper.

She wondered how he stood the lack of privacy six nights out of every seven. According to Greg, it wasn't that the Lazy Y needed to take in dudes these days, so why continue to do it? Whatever else she might consider him capable of, avarice somehow didn't fit the bill.

Called to the phone just as the two loaded minibuses

were about to set off, Cal waved them away, saying he would follow in the station wagon.

'If he doesn't decide to give it a miss altogether,' said Margot as they moved off.

'Why would he?' asked Greg.

His wife giggled. 'Probably because he suspects Madam Quincy is planning the big seduction scene, and he's none too good in the diplomatic put-down department.'

She hadn't bothered to keep her voice down. Not, thought Alex, that it was likely she wouldn't have been heard by the others occupying the vehicle. Stella Quincy was in the other bus, but that didn't mean that those present wouldn't take offence at the slur cast on one of their group. She didn't dare look round.

'Take more than diplomacy to put that one off,' said one of the men, drawing laughter all round and setting her mind at rest. 'She's been laying it on the line since we got here.'

'Looking for a lost youth,' quipped a cheerfully malicious female voice, drawing another burst of laughter. 'Can't find any fault with her taste, mind you. That brother of yours is prime beefcake!'

'Same as me,' put in her partner complacently. 'S'why you fell for me, right, hon?'

'Keep dreaming, lover!' came the ready response.

Alex joined in the general laughter, refusing to allow despondency any hold. She was going to enjoy this evening, regardless of who was or wasn't there.

They arrived at the barn-like community hall where the dance was being held in time to secure a couple of tables. Hair piled on top of her head for coolness, bare shoulders smooth and creamy, Alex was immediately the focal point of every male eye in the vicinity.

'Told you you'd have 'em all slavering in that outfit,' said Margot inelegantly. 'Cal'd better get here fast!'

'I'll stand guard till he does.' Greg returned his sister's caustic glance blandly. 'He'd do the same for me.'

Best to ignore them both, Alex decided, shelving the reply she'd been about to make. They'd realise the true state of affairs between her and Cal soon enough without her underlining it for them.

Somewhat surprisingly, the first dance announced was a waltz. Margot dragged Greg onto the floor for it, sliding her arms about his neck and looking up into his face with her heart in her eyes for all to see. To Alex, there was still more indulgence than devotion in his regard, but it seemed to be enough for her sister-in-law, so who was she to quibble? Providing he stayed around long enough for them to have the chance, Greg's feelings would deepen in time, she was sure.

Mind occupied, she only became aware of Royd's approach when he touched her elbow to attract her attention. 'Like to do this one?' he asked.

With so many eyes on the two of them she found it impossible to form a refusal. She smiled instead, and got to her feet to accompany him onto the floor, doing her best to appear at ease as he slid his arms about her.

'I guess I can't blame you for going after the boss,' he said. 'His prospects are a sight better than mine.'

'Aren't you jumping to a few too many conclusions?' Alex asked after a moment's somewhat stunned silence. 'I'm not *after* anyone!'

'The boys are betting on you against Diane Lattimer,' he went on, as if she hadn't spoken. 'There's money riding on it, so don't let 'em down.'

'If this is your idea of a joke, I'm afraid my sense of humour doesn't stretch to it,' she said crisply, deciding enough was enough. 'In fact, I think it might be a good idea if we—'

'Oh, come on!' he exclaimed. 'I was down by the corral when you waylaid him on the veranda last night. I saw him take you inside. Come up to scratch, did he?'

Alex took a hold on herself. The only way to handle innuendo of this kind was to treat it with the contempt it deserved. 'Grow up,' she said shortly.

The formerly boyish features looked anything but right now. 'I don't like being given the run-around,' he growled. 'You were all over me to start with.'

'I was *what*?' Alex could hardly believe what he was saying. 'Of all the...' She caught herself up again, aware of curious glances being directed their way. 'I think we'd better leave it right there,' she substituted tautly.

It was perhaps fortunate that the combo chose that moment to call a halt between numbers. Royd let go of her immediately, stepping back to give her a curt nod. 'Thanks for the dance.'

Alex turned and walked away without another word, nerves tensing even further on sight of Cal talking with Diane by the door. He was wearing tailored brown trousers and pale beige shirt tonight—probably the closest he ever came to formal dress.

Dark hair offset by the scarlet shirt she was wearing, Diane made an eye-catching figure too. On the face of it, she was everything he could possibly want or need in a woman, yet it still didn't appear to be enough. What chance did someone like herself stand?

'Royd looked none too happy just now,' commented Stella Quincy slyly when she reached the table. 'I guess he thought he'd got it made after the time you two spent together last night.'

'I guess a lot of people are ready to read a lot into a

little,' Alex returned coolly, and wished she hadn't as the older woman's face darkened. Ask for it though she had, she was still a guest. Alex toyed briefly with the idea of apologising, but couldn't bring herself to be that two-faced. Best to just let it pass, she decided, sliding into her seat.

Pretty as a picture in her sprigged cotton, Margot came back with Greg, her brows drawing together as she looked over to where her brother was still talking with Diane. The frown deepened as a new number was called and he allowed himself to be drawn out onto the floor. Alex kept her own expression strictly neutral, but there was no denying the pang. Jealousy plain and simple, she thought wryly.

There were too many people on the floor, this time, to keep more than a passing track of the only couple she was interested in. When they did come into view they looked to be deep in conversation. Diane's dark head upturned, hands resting on the broad shoulders, body pressed close. Cal might not have marriage in mind but he certainly wasn't indifferent to the woman. They'd been lovers, Alex was sure; probably still were on occasion.

Diane showed no inclination to rejoin her own party when the dance finished. Alex made every effort to be friendly to the girl, but found it hard going when her overtures elicited only the briefest of replies. So far as the other was concerned, there was only one person of interest at the table—and she didn't seem to care who knew it.

It was Margot who got in first when a square dance was called. 'Why don't you show Alex how to do this, Cal?' she said swiftly.

The design was blatant enough to raise flats of colour

in Alex's cheeks. That Cal recognised it too she didn't doubt, although there was little evidence of it as he lifted a dark brow in her direction.

'Like to try?'

About to decline, Alex caught Diane's supercilious little smile and abruptly changed her mind. Why make it so obvious how she felt? Her own smile was pure honey. 'I'd love to.'

She regretted the gesture as they moved out onto the floor, conscious of muscle and sinew contracting involuntarily when he slid an arm about her waist to swing her into the starting position.

'Relax,' Cal said drily. 'Just listen to the caller and follow my lead. Nobody's going to mind if you put a foot wrong.'

Putting a foot wrong was far from her major concern; keeping her emotions under control came head of the list.

She found it easier when they got under way, enjoying the lively sequences. This was how she had always visualised such occasions in her mind's eye: the swirling colours, the smiling faces, the sheer exuberance. These people had televisions in their homes, modern conveniences in their kitchens, motorised transport at their door, but they still knew the value of life's simpler pleasures.

Everything else forgotten in the sheer exhilaration of the moment, she looked up at her partner with sparkling eyes when they came to a final halt, the overhead lights catching her hair as she tilted her head, turning it to pure spun gold. 'That was terrific!'

The combo struck up one of the slower numbers they were using between sets. Cal didn't bother asking her if she wanted to do it, just drew her to him.

For the first few moments, Alex was conscious only

of physical sensation: the feel of his breath stirring her hair, the pressure of his chest against her breasts, the ripple of thigh muscle. His hands were firm at her back, long, tensile fingers slightly spread, their very touch like fire through the thin material of her blouse.

'Diane isn't going to like this,' was the only thing she could think of to say.

'I'm not answerable to Diane,' came the measured response. 'Any more than she is to me.' He looked down at her, irony in the line of his mouth. 'I've never been answerable to any woman.'

'And never intend to be, I suppose,' she retorted, pulling herself together.

'Depends whether I ever find one I can trust. I hold old-fashioned views on fidelity.'

A yardstick Diane had failed to measure up to somewhere along the line, Alex concluded.

'A two-way application, naturally,' she said, with an irony of her own.

'Where it matters, yes.'

'So much more difficult for a man, though.'

'It needn't be, with the right woman.'

'One who'll keep him fully satisfied, you mean?'

'In bed *and* out of it. A tall order, I agree, but I still live in hope.'

'In the meantime you'll settle for what you can get.'

He gave her a mocking smile. 'When it isn't snatched away from me. Maybe I made a mistake letting it go at that. Some women like the rougher approach.'

Alex bit her lip. 'You're so utterly sure of your own judgement, aren't you?' she accused in a low tone. 'Everything and everyone! Does it ever occur to you that you could possibly be wrong?'

'About you, for instance?' He paused briefly, expression far from encouraging. 'Maybe if you'd steered clear of Royd tonight I might have felt a bit more inclined to reassess. I saw the two of you dancing when I arrived.'

'You obviously didn't see the parting.'

'You didn't have to dance with him at all.'

'I was hardly going to show him up in front of the rest of the boys by refusing point-blank! Not that I need have bothered,' she added with deliberation. 'They'd already decided where my interests really lay. They'll be watching us right now, and speculating on how I'm doing.'

'Then we'd better give them something to speculate about,' he said with equal deliberation, and dropped his head to find her mouth with his, bringing up a hand to the back of her head so she couldn't drag away.

The kiss held nothing in the way of tenderness, but it still stirred her. It stirred him too; she felt it happen. She gave him a wicked little smile when he broke off, partly to cover her own ignition.

'You'd better hope the music doesn't stop too soon!'

The flash of humour in the grey eyes was unexpected. 'I'll make sure you walk in front if it does.' He studied her, expression undergoing an indefinable alteration. 'Maybe we should start over.'

Alex felt her heart give an almighty jerk. It took everything she had to keep her voice level. 'Are you capable of keeping an open mind?'

'Like I told you before, I'm open to persuasion,' he said. 'Though you'd have to be a great deal better at it than your brother's been to date.'

'You can hardly say he's neglecting Margot tonight,' she protested.

'It's early yet.'

'I could have a word with him,' she suggested weakly, sensing his rejection even before he answered.

'If he needs to be told to pay his wife more attention, the interest isn't there to start with.'

Alex hardly felt able to argue with that assessment. After what Greg had admitted to her yesterday morning, sibling loyalty was in pretty short supply altogether.

'I think, given a choice, Margot would opt for the lesser hurt,' she said slowly. 'While he's still here, there's still hope of his coming to feel more for her.'

'At least you've given up trying to convince me he already does.'

Blue eyes met grey unswervingly. 'I've given up trying to convince myself. It isn't that he doesn't care for her at all, just that he—'

'Just that he doesn't love her the way she deserves to be loved.' The lean features had hardened again. 'You're saying I should leave it at that?'

'If you don't want to cause Margot a whole lot of heartache. I know it's a cliché, but it's better to have half a loaf rather than none at all.'

Cal regarded her dispassionately. 'Is that your own view?'

'No,' she admitted. 'But it isn't me we're talking about.' She hesitated before saying more, afraid of undoing any good she might have done, but finally went on, 'They only have the evenings and days off to be together any length of time. If you put Greg in charge of guest activities they could share a lot more.'

'You've got it all figured out, haven't you?' he said. He shook his head as she opened her mouth to respond, expression still giving little away. 'I'll think about it.'

The combo came to the end of the number. Cal released her, the corners of his mouth twitching as she gave an involuntary glance downwards. 'All under control.'

'I never really doubted it,' she said, furious with herself for blushing, and saw the twitch widen into a genuine, reassuring grin.

'Nice to know.'

To Alex, it was both a surprise and a relief, on reaching the table, to find Diane's chair empty. She hadn't looked forward to seeing her reaction.

'She left when the two of you started smooching,' advised Margot with open satisfaction. 'Nose right out of joint! Not the only one either,' she added, lower-toned, with a glance in Stella Quincy's direction. 'Talk about green-eyed envy! She's been fancying Cal since she got here.'

Cal had gone to talk to those occupying the other table, his lean length standing easy, a foot hoisted to the lower rail of a chair. Alex dragged her eyes away from him with an effort and found Greg watching her, an odd little smile on his lips.

'Glad you came?' he asked.

'Of course,' she said lightly. 'It's good to see you again after all this time.'

'We're going to make the most of your being here, aren't we, sweetie?' He slung an arm about his wife's slender shoulders.

'The very most,' she agreed. 'You'll never want to go home!'

She felt that way already, Alex could have told her. Especially now. Start over, Cal had said: a chance to make him see her as she wanted him to see her. As Greg had pulled out all the stops to get Margot to fall for him, so she would do the same. Whatever it took!

Cal danced only twice more during the rest of the

evening: once with one of the female guests, whose partner expressed a reluctance to get up at all, the other with
Stella Quincy who made it impossible, short of downright rudeness, to refuse.

The latter had deliberately chosen one of the slower
numbers, but had received little joy from the contact, if
her expression on her return to the table was anything
to go by. Put down in no uncertain terms, Alex judged,
viewing the line of Cal's mouth. There had to be a limit
on how much he would allow even a guest to get away
with.

Not short of other partners herself, Alex made every
effort to appear unruffled by his failure to ask her again.
Once or twice she caught him watching her appraisingly,
as if still weighing her up, but for the most part he talked
and acted as if nothing was different between them. So
far nothing was, she supposed. Trust had to be gained.

Time was called on the dancing at midnight, but it
was another twenty minutes before the Lazy Y party
finally emerged into the refreshing coolness of the night
air. The sky was clear, the stars so bright they seemed
larger than normal. Lack of pollution, Alex surmised.
Deep breathing was no hazard to health out here.

Cal came up behind her as she trailed in the wake of
the group making for the waiting transport.

'How about keeping me company?' he suggested.

'Why?' she asked, fighting the urge to grab at the
offer.

His lips slanted. 'We need to talk.'

It was on the tip of her tongue to say About what?
but that would be too dangerously close to the game-
playing he despised. 'I should let the others know, or
they'll be wondering where I got to,' she said instead.

'No problem, we've already been seen.'

The station wagon was parked some short distance away. He put her into the passenger seat before going round to slide behind the wheel, firing the ignition with a flick of a wrist and setting straight off. Margot waved from the minibus window as they passed.

It was further to Prescott by road, Alex had realised on the way out earlier in the day, although roughly the same in actual travelling time. Cal made no immediate attempt to start a conversation. Stealing a glance at the lean, clean-cut profile, she wondered what was really going on inside that dark head. Little more than twenty-four hours ago she had been in his arms. If she hadn't pulled back...

'I gather you're no longer a shining light in Mrs Quincy's eyes?' she said, desperate for something, anything, to get the ball rolling.

'Not even a glimmer,' he agreed.

Alex would have loved to know just what he had said to the woman, but doubted if he would be prepared to tell her. 'I feel so sorry for her husband,' she added. 'He obviously knows what's going on.'

'Then he should do something about it,' came the unequivocal reply. 'Anyway, forget about the Quincys. They'll be gone in the morning.'

'Don't you ever get fed-up with having guests constantly around the place?' she asked after a moment.

The broad shoulders lifted in a brief shrug. 'It can get a bit wearing at times, but it's kept us in the black these last few years. It's given Margot the opportunity to meet folk from other parts too—even other countries. We've been all American this week, but we get other nationalities coming in from time to time. English included. There's one due in this next week, as a matter of fact.'

Unlikely that she'd be recognised, Alex assured herself, refusing to panic. Anyway, she had other concerns right now.

'About last night,' she said, taking the bull by the horns before she lost courage. 'I can appreciate how it must have looked.'

His expression didn't alter. 'So how was it?'

'The way you took it for granted that I'd played the same scene before—many times before, in fact. It... Well, it caught me on the raw, that's all. I don't sleep around, Cal. I never have.'

It was a moment or two before he answered, eyes on the road ahead. When he did speak it was on a level note. 'What about earlier?'

'You mean heading right back to Royd?' She made a rueful gesture. 'Similar thing. You rubbed me up the wrong way.'

There was a hint of humour in the brief widening of his lips. 'Nothing to what I had in mind if Margot hadn't called us over. That act you pulled was sure asking for it!' His tone altered, taking on a wry quality. 'I guess I had you tagged before you even got here. Maybe as much due to your brother as what you do for a living.'

'*Did*,' she corrected. 'I'd already made the decision before I came out.'

'That's not what you said at supper.'

'I know. Greg rather dropped it on me.'

'So what *do* you have planned?'

'Nothing concrete as yet, but I've enough money put by to see me through a few months while I look round.'

'What was it made you decide to make it a total break?' he asked. 'Even if work wasn't coming so easy, I'd have thought it better to wait till it wasn't coming at all before pulling out.'

For a moment, Alex was tempted to tell him the truth,

but only for a moment. The chance of his believing her side of the story was remote. 'I was tired of the whole scene,' she said instead. 'I want to live a normal life, with a steady job and friends I can rely on.'

'Marriage and kids too?'

Her heart jerked. 'If it's meant to be, yes. I'm no different from most other women in that respect.'

'You're not like any other woman I ever knew,' came the dry comment. 'There seems to be several different people tied up in there.'

'Stand up the real Alex Sherwood!' she quipped, not all that sure that she knew herself.

Cal made no immediate answer. They were coming up to a minor crossroads. Instead of carrying straight through, on the main road, he turned right, heading down what wasn't much more than a lane.

'Short cut,' he said, sensing her unspoken question. 'Not suitable for the buses.'

Not really suitable for anything but a four-wheel drive, she thought as the road surface deteriorated by the yard. The moonlight was bright enough to reveal wide open space to either side, with the mountains a dark mass up ahead. Apart from a faint glow in the sky way over on the right where Prescott lay, there was no sign of human habitation.

'It's all so vast!' she murmured. 'We have open countryside in England, but nothing on this scale.'

'Missing city life?' The question was soft.

She shook her head. 'It never held all that much appeal to start with. A square peg in a round hole all the way through!'

Another man might have made some trite play on the word square, as applied to her shape. Cal gave a faint grin but let it pass. 'Feeling like that, you're right to get out,' he said. 'It still leaves the question of what you're going to do as an alternative.'

'I could possibly get a job as a riding instructress,' she suggested lightly.

'Are there many openings in that line?'

'It's a popular sport, so there must be some.' With little opportunity for the unqualified, came the mental rider. 'Something will turn up,' she added, reluctant even to think about the sales job right now. 'I shan't starve.'

Cal made no attempt to pursue the subject any further. A moment later he pulled up and got out to open a gate, closing it again after driving through and heading along a track that shone white in the moonlight.

To Alex, the ranch land alone seemed limitless. Eight thousand acres to call home: a world within a world. She had never wanted anything more than she wanted to be a part of that world.

They crossed a wooden bridge over a loop of the river, topping a slight rise to see the homestead lights twinkling in the distance. Another ten minutes' driving, Alex reckoned. They'd beat the buses back without a doubt.

As if in direct response to the thought, Cal brought the car to a stop, turning off both ignition and lights. The blood sang in her ears as he put out a hand to slide the scarf she was using as a wrap from her shoulders, reaching a crescendo when the same hand curved the back of her neck to draw her towards him. This was what she had been waiting for—what she had hoped for—why she was here at all.

The kiss started slow and gentle, lips brushing hers, teasing them apart with a delicacy that sent shudder after delicious shudder through her body. His hands were warm on her bare shoulders, smoothing over and down her arms to slide beneath the stretched top of her blouse and lower it all the way.

She wore nothing beneath, her breasts firm enough to have no need of support. He cupped them both in his hands, holding back for a moment to look, to admire, the expression in his eyes a reflection of what Alex was feeling all the way through.

'Every inch a revelation!' he murmured. 'If you knew the struggle I had to act the gentleman when you came out of that shower the other night!'

'I don't remember much of the gentleman,' Alex said softly.

'I put a towel round you, didn't I? Compared with what I wanted to do, that was pure chivalry.'

He lowered his head to run the very tip of his tongue around one aureole, closing in to take her hardened, aching nipple in his mouth and create mayhem throughout her whole body.

Head jerked backwards in a rictus of sensation, Alex wove her fingers into the crisp, clean thickness of the dark hair. Her mind was floating, her senses concentrated on the sensual movement of his lips and tongue, the tumult inside her gathering strength with every passing second.

Her breath dried in her throat when he lifted his head to kiss her lightly on the lips before drawing the blouse back up again, the deprivation almost too much to bear.

'Any more and I'll not be able to stop,' he said softly. 'If we're going to make love, let's give ourselves the time and the space to enjoy it the way it should be enjoyed.' He brought up a hand and smoothed the back of his fingers down her cheek, tilting her chin to look into her eyes, his gaze penetrating what little defence she had left against him. 'We are going to make love.'

It was more statement than question, but she had no quarrel with that. Whatever he wanted, she wanted too. She kissed the thumb he rubbed across her lips and saw the firm mouth stretch into a slow, stomach-curling smile.

'Home,' he said.

CHAPTER EIGHT

THE minibuses were back and already disgorging their passengers when they reached the house. Cal let Alex out before putting the car away in the outbuilding that served as a garage, leaving her to face a regular barrage of speculative glances as she made her way indoors.

Margot caught her up as she mounted the stairs, viewing her with an impish sparkle. 'Cal behave himself, did he?'

'Like a gentleman.' Alex congratulated herself on her light and easy tone. 'What time do people start leaving tomorrow?'

'Today, you mean,' her sister-in-law corrected. 'Right after breakfast—although we'll be having it a bit later than usual to compensate for the late night. Leaves the rest of the day for the cabins to be turned round ready for the new lot on Monday.'

They had reached the stair-head. Alex paused, an ear tuned for the sound of Cal's voice among those still audible from outside. 'I'm more than willing to lend a hand with the turn-around.'

'Not necessary, thanks. We bring in extra people. You just have a nice, relaxing day.'

'I'll do that.' Alex gave the younger girl a smile. 'See you at breakfast, then.'

Safely in her room, she leaned against the door for a moment to gather herself, pulses quickening afresh as she viewed the double bed. The time and the space, Cal had said. He would come as soon as the house was quiet—and she would be ready for him this time. She was ready right now, limbs turning to jelly at the mere thought of lying in those strong arms, held close against that lean, hard body.

She undressed quickly, sliding between the sheets to lie gazing at the shadowed ceiling. How long would he wait? she wondered as the minutes ticked by. Why wait at all, in fact? They were two adult people indulging a mutual desire. The way Margot had been going on, she was more likely to be delighted than shocked if she knew.

What *she* mustn't do was read more into Cal's feelings for her than actually existed, she told herself. He wanted her, yes, but that was as far as it went at present. Getting him to trust her was a first priority.

It was an hour before she finally accepted that he wasn't coming at all: one long hour before it dawned on her that this was his retaliation for last night. He'd been playing her along the whole time with this in mind, she thought desolately. The suggestion that they start again, the invitation to join him in the car instead of taking the bus—every single thing he had done to her back there—it had all been planned.

And how easy she had made it for him! He must have been laughing like a drain inside at her gullibility. Her cheeks burned at the memory of his hands and lips on her body. She would have given him anything he had asked of her right then and he had known it. She supposed she should be grateful that he'd had the decency to leave her that much.

She dozed from time to time during the hours following, but it was there immediately every time she opened her eyes. The thought of facing him again, of seeing the cynical amusement in the grey eyes was unbearable, but there was no way round it. Her only recourse, she decided in the end, was to act as if nothing at all had happened between them. That way, she at least salvaged something of her pride.

Wide awake at six, she made a cautious foray to the bathroom. Cal's door was closed, all silent within. It was still closed when she came back after taking a shower, but she could hear movement now.

Back in her room, she pulled on a pair of jeans and a shirt, sliding her feet into the heeled boots without thinking about it. The deep ache wouldn't go away, but she could cope with it. Under no circumstances was she going to let Cal see her beaten down, she told herself fiercely.

She could hear water gushing when she passed the bathroom again. So much for his claim not to have known anyone was in there that first night! Wearing nothing but a pair of pyjama bottoms, Greg emerged from the room opposite as she started down the stairs, greeting her with a lazy grin.

'It's Sunday,' he said. 'We're all allowed a bit of a lie-in.'

'I can't stay in bed once I'm awake,' Alex claimed, and saw the grin come again.

'Depends whether there's anything worth staying in for. Marriage has some compensations!'

'More than enough in your case,' she returned on a crisper note. 'You're a lucky man, Greg. A whole lot luckier than you deserve to be! Try remembering it.'

She carried on down before he could answer, in no mood to pull any punches where her brother was concerned. He had a wife who adored him, a good home and job—what more did he want?

Some of the guests were already out and about, taking

advantage of the extra hour before breakfast to enjoy a
last look around. Alex joined a small group saying good-
bye to the horses in the corral. Jingo was among them
and in a good mood, coming across to nuzzle the fingers
she stretched out to him.

'We heard he took off with you Friday,' commented
one of the men, watching her stroke the soft nose. 'He
looks quiet enough right now.'

'He likes to lull people into a sense of false security.'
She smiled. 'Have you enjoyed your week?'

'Sure. First real working ranch we've tried so far.
Must be a big change for you,' he added. 'I'll bet you
can't wait to get back to the bright lights!'

Alex murmured some appropriate response, striving
to contain the welling despondency. Come Thursday, if
not before, she would be on her way. Between times she
had to come up with some plausible reason for cutting
her visit short.

Cal was out on the veranda with the rest of the guests
when they eventually went back up to the house. His
greeting encompassed them all. Only too sure of what
she would see there, Alex avoided any direct confron-
tation with the grey eyes, joining in the general conversation around her. She could feel him looking at her
from time to time but he made no effort to draw her
attention. Then, why should he need to? The message
had already been delivered.

If asked afterwards, she couldn't have said what she
ate at breakfast. She was just glad when the meal was
over. Luggage was already being loaded into the minibuses for the journey into Sheridan when she got outside.
Some of the guests had planes to catch, others their cars
to pick up, all of them a lengthy journey to contemplate—and tomorrow it would all begin again.

The need to be on her own for a while drove Alex to the barn to pick up a saddle. With all the milling around back there, she calculated she could be up and away before anyone noticed she was gone. The mountains beckoned. A couple of hours communing with nature would put things in perspective. No man was worth getting into a state over.

Mounted on the chestnut mare she had ridden that first time, she headed for the slopes without a backward glance. Her hat was back in her room, but it wasn't essential. Her hair was both thick enough and long enough to shield her from the sun.

Fifteen minutes brought her into the foothills. She left it to Minty to choose one of the many trails, content to just meander along through the aspen and cottonwood cloaking the lower slopes, drinking in the scenery—allowing the peace and solitude to soothe her wounded vanity.

Because that was all it really was, when it was boiled down. She had made herself available and been given the cold shoulder. At least he'd done it before and not after. Such fortitude in a man had to be admired.

Bastard! she thought, and felt better for it.

It was going on for noon when she finally and reluctantly started back, once again leaving it to Minty to find the way. The occasional bird call and the constant humming of insects were the only sounds to break the tranquillity. Other than a glimpse through the trees of what she had taken to be a small herd of deer, she had seen scarcely any animal-life at all.

As if in direct response to the thought, Minty gave a sudden whinny and picked up her pace, startling Alex into taking a firmer grasp on the rein. The mare had scented something, it was obvious. Couldn't be anything

dangerous, though, or she'd hardly be forging ahead so
eagerly.

It was something of a shock, on rounding the bend in
the trail, to see Cal sitting there on Jed. Face set, he
made no move as Alex walked the mare slowly towards
him. She could see the angry glitter in his eyes from
several yards away.

'Just what kind of game are you playing?' he jerked
out.

'Game?' Alex lifted her brows as if genuinely surprised by the question. 'I felt like a ride, that's all.'

'Without letting anybody know where you were going!'

'*You* obviously knew,' she countered.

'I tracked you.'

'Really? I thought the Indians were the only ones who
could do that!'

'I was taught by an Indian,' he said shortly. 'You
shouldn't be up here at all without company. Apart from
anything else, there's no horse can be guaranteed not to
act up if it scents bear—and there's plenty around this
time of year.'

'Rattlesnakes too!' she flashed, giving way to an impulse she immediately regretted as she saw a certain en-
lightenment dawn in the grey eyes.

'Is that why you took off?' he asked on a somewhat
milder note. 'Because I stayed away from you last
night?'

She had left herself wide open to that, Alex acknowledged. It was too late for denials but she still felt bound
to make the attempt, lifting her shoulders in a shrug
meant to convey indifference. 'I "took off", as you put
it, because I fancied a ride, no other reason.'

'Then why the acid?' He moved Jed just enough to

block her passage as she attempted to ride past, shaking his head. 'You're not going anywhere till we've sorted this out.'

'There's nothing to sort!' she insisted. 'We're even. Just leave it at that.'

'You really think I set you up to get my own back for the night before?' His laugh made a mockery of the idea. 'Revenge might be sweet, honey, but not *that* sweet! I'd have been there like a shot if I hadn't got called out.'

Alex gazed at him with an arrested expression. 'Called out?'

'One of the boys found a section of the perimeter fence cut through. We were out there till gone five waiting. I heard you in the bathroom when I got in, but I wasn't in any state right then to do either of us justice.'

'Did you catch anybody?' It was all Alex could come up with for the moment.

'Nobody turned up. Probably realised they'd been spotted.'

'But you've had no sleep at all?'

He gave a dry smile. 'I was planning on snatching a couple of hours after everybody went, till you decided otherwise.'

'I'm sorry.' She put up a shaky hand and pushed it through her hair, aware of having made a complete fool of herself. 'I thought you were gloating about it.'

'Considering the way you wouldn't even look at me this morning, I was having a few doubts of my own,' Cal admitted. 'You can switch moods faster than any other woman I ever met!'

'I'll try to be more consistent,' she promised.

'It would make life easier.' His lips widened briefly. 'On the other hand, it would be a whole lot duller.'

He studied her for a moment, gaze roving the tousled

mane of blonde hair, the sculpted cheekbones and softly curved mouth—eyes meeting hers with an expression that set her heart thudding against her ribcage, the spark dividing and multiplying as he registered the response she couldn't hide.

He dismounted in one smooth movement, sticking his hat over the saddle-horn and slapping Jed on the rump to send him away, then coming over to hold up his hands in invitation.

Alex kicked her feet free of the stirrups and slid down into his arms, leaning back against the lean, hard body as he kissed the side of her neck, nerves quivering, insides turning molten as heat flushed through her. His hands slid up from her waist to cup her breasts, lifting and caressing, the touch of his tongue on the sensitive inner rim of her ear like fire and ice at one and the same time.

She closed her eyes when he turned her about, kissing him feverishly, wantonly, lips forming soundless, mindless words against his, body straining to be closer still, moulding to the masculine shape.

Cal said something softly and swung her up in his arms, carried her a short distance to lay her down on a grassy patch. Sunlight dappled his features, catching the fire in his eyes. Alex lay, quiescent, as he opened her shirt—lifting her back to facilitate its removal, along with the brief brassière. He took one peaking, aching nipple in his mouth, teasing it with his tongue to even greater prominence, sucking hard one moment, then soft, driving her wild with a pleasure so intense it was almost pain.

'*Enough!*' she heard herself pleading. 'No more, Cal!'

He laughed low in his throat and said softly, 'You don't mean that.'

She didn't either. Her whole body craved his touch. She unbuttoned his own shirt, tugging it free of his jeans and pushing it back from his shoulders to run her hands over the firm musculature, thrilling to the power contained there. His biceps were hard as iron, filling her palms the way her breasts filled his, pulsing beneath her fingers. She traced a slow passage across his chest with her fingertips, following the line of bone, the ridging of muscle, feeling the strong beat of his heart and hearing his breathing roughen.

He pulled her closer so that their bodies touched, bare skin against bare skin. His hands played over her back to plunge into the thickness of her hair, fingers stroking her nape, mouth moving softly, tantalisingly, on hers, arousing a desire so fierce it was like being torn apart.

She felt his hands move the full length of her body to remove her boots, the suppleness of his fingers unbuckling the belt of her jeans. They slid away easily, along with the brief panties she wore beneath, leaving her fully exposed to his gaze. It wasn't the first time he'd seen her nude but this was so different, his expression, as he studied her, lacking any hint of cynicism, his hands almost reverent in their exploratory passage over waist and hip.

The muscles of her inner thighs spasmed as he splayed his fingers over her lower abdomen. He bent again to kiss her, tongue sliding silkily between her parted lips, fingertips cool against her heated flesh, making her writhe and gasp in mind-blowing delirium.

Eyes slitted, body trembling, she watched him unbuckle his belt with one-handed dexterity, spasming again on sight of him. Then he was over and above her, pressuring her thighs apart with a gentle knee to bring his potent weight to bear, the incursion slow, measured, the feeling exquisite.

Alex slid her hands down to grasp taut twin hemispheres, a moan dragged from deep in her throat as he filled her. For a moment he was still, watching her face, the flame in his eyes a reflection of that consuming her. When he started to move it was gently at first, pacing himself, increasing the tempo as the hunger mounted in them both, breath coming faster and rougher in tune with her own, tension stretching to unbearable limits.

She was lost in a world of pure sensation, her body arching to meet him, face etched with passion. She cried out wildly when the coiled spring inside her finally snapped, the sound mingling with Cal's hoarse shout as he let go the iron-willed control.

It took a snort from one of the horses to bring her out of the hazy, lazy aftermath. Cal had rolled to one side, leaving an arm thrown heavily across her waist. His eyes were closed, giving her a rare chance to study the lean features in close-up, appraising the taut stretch of tanned skin over hard, masculine cheekbones, the straight jut of his nose and firm line of jaw. That strongly moulded, wonderfully shaped mouth had given her so much pleasure. She put out a tentative hand to touch it, heart jerking as he caught the fingertip between his lips.

'I thought you were asleep,' she murmured.

'Recuperating,' he said. The grey eyes came open, stirring her blood once more with their expressive gleam. 'You're a pretty exhausting lady!' He slid a hand up from her waist to her breast, the caress both familiar and possessive. 'Sleep's the last thing on my mind.'

With her body already reacting to the subtle movement of his fingers, it was the last thing she was thinking of too, right now. 'I never realised it could be like that,' she whispered.

The smile was brief. 'Pretty good for the ego too!'

'It's true.' Alex held his gaze, willing him to believe her. 'You gave me the most pleasure I ever had in my life!'

Something in him seemed to give a little, his expression softening. 'You did a fair job yourself.'

She put on a mock pout. 'Only fair?'

He laughed, taking her hand and guiding it to him. 'Total demolition good enough for you?'

'I dare say you'll soon bounce back,' she said, doing her best to emulate his lack of self-consciousness.

He viewed the faint colour in her cheeks with an expression suddenly very close to tenderness replacing the amusement. Releasing her hand, he slid his arm about her to draw her closer, kissing her on the tip of her small, straight nose. 'You're beautiful,' he said softly. 'All the way through! I—'

Whatever it was he'd been about to say was lost as Alex gave an involuntary yell at the sudden red-hot stab in her left buttock. Jerking upright, she swatted the wasp-like insect away from her, rubbing furiously at the burning, reddened patch. 'That lousy creature stung me!'

There was no response from the man still lying at her side. When she looked down at him he was shaking with silent laughter, lower lip clutched between his teeth.

'It isn't funny!' she shot at him indignantly. 'It darn well hurt!'

'I know,' he gasped. 'Like fury!' He pressed himself upright, leaning on an elbow to survey the wound, lips still quivering. 'Vinegar's the best remedy. Unfortunately, I don't carry any round with me.'

'Thanks for the sympathy!' she snapped, still in too much pain to see anything remotely humorous about it.

'Well, if you will lie around the woods bare-assed,' he said, 'What can you expect?'

Realisation cut the scathing retort off at source, the heatwave surging over her like a riptide. Her rear-end wasn't the only part of her on show.

'I never knew a blush could extend so far,' Cal observed with interest as she looked round wildly for her clothing.

'Shut up!' she snarled, then caught his eye and felt her anger dissolve as the bubble finally burst, her scowl giving way to a wry smile. 'I notice you took good care not to expose too much of *your* ass,' she said, and immediately blushed again as he lifted an expressive eyebrow.

'I'll make a point of it next time.'

'You're planning on there being a next time?' she asked softly.

His regard hardened a fraction. 'Aren't you?'

'Is it up to me?' she countered, and saw his mouth turn down at the corner.

'Don't try playing the submissive role, it doesn't suit you. Bores the pants off me into the bargain,' he added drily.

'Anything you say,' she rejoined, straight-faced.

Humour re-established itself. 'Guess I asked for that.'

He was silent for a moment, just looking at her as she sat there, skin dappled by the filtered sunlight, the expression growing in his eyes stirring her anew. 'How's the sting?' he asked softly.

'Better,' she confirmed, unsurprised to hear the huskiness in her voice. 'Shouldn't we be getting back?'

'Probably.' He reached out and drew her to him, the

kiss gentle, then put her away again, jaw firming. 'In fact, definitely, before they send a search party out after the pair of us.'

Raking the scattered clothing together within easy reach, he donned his shirt, then got to his feet to zip up his trousers and fasten his belt while she struggled into her jeans. 'I'll go get the horses.'

The two of them had wandered a short way down the trail and were peacefully cropping grass. By the time he returned with them, Alex was fully dressed and on her feet, though not by any means fully recovered.

She ran her eyes over him as he walked the two horses towards her, visualising the lean, hard body beneath the clothing—the thighs packed with muscular power from a lifetime in the saddle. He had been a part of her just now, their bodies joined as one. She yearned to know that sense of total belonging again.

'Something wrong?' Cal asked when she took Minty's rein from him. 'You're looking very pensive.'

'You didn't use anything,' she said, having just this moment thought about it.

'I wasn't carrying anything.' He paused, then added on a slightly altered note, 'Is it important?'

'You seemed to consider it vital the other night,' she murmured.

'A habit we're advised to foster regardless,' came the dry return, 'Though not always possible to put into practice. Anyway, that wasn't what I was asking. I take it *you're* protected?'

It took a moment to sink in, another to find an adequate reply. 'You don't need to worry.'

'That's okay, then.' He caught her by the arm as she made to lift her foot to the stirrup, drawing her to him. 'One for the road.'

The kiss left her both breathless and temporarily diverted. Cal was smiling when he lifted his head. 'I'll give you a leg-up.'

Seated, Alex gathered the rein and held Minty in check until Cal was settled in the saddle too, falling in behind as he turned the stallion homewards. Unbelievably, she hadn't given a thought to the possibility of pregnancy until he had mentioned it. She had gone on the Pill for that one brief period when she had believed she had found her Mr Right, and come off it again immediately she had discovered her mistake. Since then, there had been no need for precautions.

She should be all right, she calculated. She was supposed to be in her least fertile period at present. She could only hope the so-called safe period really was.

Cal waited for her to come abreast when they hit open range, directing a quizzical glance when she stayed silent.

'Tired?' he asked, with a hint of a smile on his lips.

'Not nearly as much as you must be,' she rejoined, on as light a note as she could manage. 'Good thing it's Sunday. You'll have time to catch up.'

'I'll need to,' he acknowledged. 'We'll be out again tonight.'

Alex hid her disappointment with an effort. 'Is there really any chance they might risk another attempt?'

'Depends what scared them off in the first place. The fence is still down, and the herd hasn't been moved, so we'll just wait and see.'

'I'll come out with you,' she said, the images already forming in her mind's eye. 'My night vision is pretty good.'

'No way!' His tone was emphatic. 'You don't leave the house—tonight or any other night! Do you hear me?'

'I could scarcely fail to hear you,' she retorted with some asperity. 'Why not?'

'Because I say so!'

'That's not good enough!'

'It had better be.'

'I'm not one of your men!' she challenged.

'I'm well aware of it. You're still not coming.'

Alex gave an exasperated sigh. 'You just have to be top dog, don't you?'

'Not in every instance.'

She shot him a glance, registering the glint of laughter in his eyes, the quirk at the corners of his mouth—unable to keep her flag flying in the face of it.

'You're impossible!' she declared ruefully.

'Cautious,' he corrected. 'Cattle-rustling is big business, attracting some pretty ruthless operators. I'm not prepared to take any risks.' He ran a soothing hand down Jed's neck as the stallion shied away from something sensed in the long grass. 'Steady, boy! It's only a gopher.'

Who would have thought she could ever be jealous of a horse? thought Alex wryly, aching for the feel of those hands on her own body again. It would be easy—all too easy—to let herself fall in love with this man, but what were the chances of his returning the emotion? Wanting was a long way from loving—especially for a man.

One thing was certain. If she left on Thursday, as she had planned, she would never know what might have come of it. There was nothing to stop her from cancelling the reservation. No one else even knew she had made it.

CHAPTER NINE

THERE were remonstrations from Margot for worrying the life out of her by riding off into the wild blue yonder without so much as a word.

'If Cal hadn't been able to track you, we'd have had no idea where you'd gone,' she scolded. 'Just supposing you'd been thrown and injured! You could have been lying up there for days!'

'All's well that ends well,' said Greg, a sly little smile on his face as he looked from his sister to the man at her rear. 'You must be ravenous after all that effort!'

If Cal was aware of the innuendo, he wasn't rising to it. 'Not unduly,' he returned. 'I can wait till supper. How about you, Alex?'

She shook her head. 'I'm not hungry, either, thanks.'

'Right, then, I'll go and get my head down for a couple of hours. Anything crops up, handle it,' he added to his brother-in-law. 'Practice for you.'

He was gone before the younger man could voice any question. 'What's he on about?' Greg demanded of Alex, as though she should know if anyone did. 'Practice for what?'

'Handling responsibility, I assume,' she said carefully. 'I think he might be considering letting you run the guest side.'

Her brother came upright in his chair, face lit. 'This is your doing, isn't it? You talked him round!'

'It was only a suggestion,' she denied. 'And don't count your chickens before it's properly confirmed.'

'Cal wouldn't have said it if he hadn't already decided,' declared Margot with authority. 'His whole attitude's changed since you got here, Alex. You must be a good influence!'

'And some!' Greg looked more animated than at any time since her arrival. 'I can handle the guests okay. Nothing surer!'

'*We* can handle the guests okay,' corrected his wife. 'We're going to be doing this together.'

There was no adverse reaction to that statement that Alex could see, although her brother could match Cal at times when it came to concealing his thoughts. She still wasn't a hundred percent certain that Cal meant to go the whole hog—yet, as Margot had said, why make the remark at all if he still had reservations? It was up to Greg now. If he proved himself worthy of the trust, they might even begin to forge some kind of relationship.

'I knew you'd come through for me,' he said a little later, when Margot left the two of them on their own for a few minutes. 'No man on earth could resist a plea from those big blue eyes!'

'Was that your only reason for bringing me out here?' Alex asked after a moment. 'So that I could work on Cal on your behalf?'

'Not the *only* reason, but it did cross my mind that you'd be a useful ally,' he admitted. 'I needed *some* support.'

'You had all of Margot's.'

'She doesn't hold the same kind of sway.' The blue eyes were bland. 'He was a hell of a long time fetching you back.'

'I'd gone a hell of a long way,' she responded tartly. 'Whatever you're thinking, forget it!'

'Methinks thou protesteth too much,' he came back

softly. 'Why deny it? It's been obvious from the first what was going to happen between you two. Talk about the sparks flying. Like Vesuvius in full eruption!'

'You're talking rot,' she said. 'You always did talk a lot of rot!'

'Lie to yourself if you like,' he returned derisively, 'but don't try convincing me that nothing happened out there today. You looked like a woman looks when she's been thoroughly satiated. I should know,' he added on a complacent note.

'You should hope!' Alex had already started for the door. 'I'm going up to change.'

'Don't exhaust the man totally,' Greg winged after her. 'We don't want him falling asleep when we're out tonight.'

Distracted, she turned back to look at him. 'You're standing watch too?'

'That's what I was told earlier. Might be different now I've got the guests to see to tomorrow. They're not going to be impressed by a bleary-eyed welcome party.'

'I told you not to count on it as a certainty,' Alex cautioned. 'Even if he does intend you to take over, it might not be right away.'

She made her escape before he could say anything else. Cal's door was closed when she passed it—all silent within. Not that she would have considered disturbing him for *any* purpose, much less what Greg had been suggesting.

In her room, she took a look in the mirror, wondering if it really was possible to tell when a woman had been made love to. The imprint of Cal's lips still lingered on hers, the deep-down ache was still there in her body, but there were no outward signs that she could see. Just a guess on her brother's part, she decided wryly, confirmed for him by her reaction. Hopefully, he would hold back on any further comment—especially in Cal's hearing. She would hate the latter to think her a kiss-and-tell merchant.

Tired herself, now she came to think about it, she saw no reason not to take advantage of what was left of the afternoon for some rest and recuperation of her own. She had never seen into Cal's room, so had no idea where his bed would be situated, but lying there she could imagine him bare inches away through the partition wall, long body stretched face-down on top of the covers, muscles relaxed, face in repose.

It would be wonderful, she thought, just to lie at his side watching him. Except that she wouldn't be able to resist touching him, kissing that mouth of his until he woke and responded, then feeling his arms come around her, drawing her close, making them one flesh again. She had never realised what that really meant until now. One flesh; one whole.

She wasn't in danger of falling in love with him, she already was in love with him—tied by threads he had woven about her heart and mind as well as her body. A man of integrity, that was Cal Forrester: a man to put her trust in, to rely on. Whatever it took to make him feel the same way about her, she would do it, she thought resolutely. She couldn't contemplate life without him.

It being Sunday, and the one evening they would be eating on their own as a family, she put on one of the two dresses she had bothered to bring with her. A sleeveless silk-knit tube in pale cream, it skimmed her body to mid-thigh, leaving a long expanse of shapely, lightly tanned bare leg on show. Cal was no different from other men when it came to visual impact. If her looks were the main appeal at present, then she was going to use them to full advantage.

He was seated, alone, out on the veranda when she went down, feet raised to the rail in the casual manner that so suited his style, chair tipped back, hands clasped behind his head. He looked her over appreciatively as she leaned against the rail by his feet.

'You look good enough to eat!'

'With or without mustard?' Alex asked flippantly, giving vent to a startled gasp as chair and feet went down and she was seized about the hips to be drawn onto his knees for a long, demanding kiss.

'Stop it!' she breathed when he finally let her up for air, catching the fingers sliding along her bare thigh. 'The others will be here any minute!'

Cal laughed, eyes teasing. 'If you didn't want me to touch, you shouldn't have worn it. You've the longest, loveliest pair of legs I ever saw!' He ran his hand down her side, following the curve of breast and waist and hip. 'A body to drive any man crazy!'

'Is that all you see in me?' she said, on what she hoped was a suitably bantering note, and saw the teasing light replaced by something far less easily read.

'I've still to get to grips with the rest.' He made no attempt to detain her as she started hastily to her feet at the sound of Margot's voice, regarding her with a dry smile as she sank into the nearest chair. 'Given the opportunity.'

'Opportunity for what?' asked his sister, emerging from the house in time to catch the last.

'Some questions you don't ask,' admonished Greg, following behind. 'Still got a terrific pair of pins, I see, sis!' he added blithely.

'Terrific everything,' sighed his wife. 'I'd love to be tall!'

If ever there was a cue for some husbandly reassurance this was it, Alex reflected, annoyed with Greg for failing to respond. He still had a long way to go when it came to understanding the female psyche. She could feel Cal's eyes on her still, but didn't dare to look at him directly for fear of giving too much away. Greg wasn't the only one with a long way to go as yet.

Cal waited until supper was over before finally confirming the new arrangement with his brother-in-law.

'The boys will pitch in where necessary,' he said, 'but you'll be directly responsible for all the organisation and guest welfare from now on.'

'No problem,' Greg assured him. He paused briefly and added gruffly, 'And thanks.'

The darker head inclined. 'Just do a good job and we'll all be happy. You've a ten o'clock pick-up to make, so you'd better stay home tonight.'

Alex wished they were both staying home. At least last night she hadn't been aware of any danger. If another attempt was made, Cal wasn't going to be doing any holding back while someone went for the law.

He left at ten-thirty along with four of the hands. Watching them go, Alex thought wistfully that there were times when being a woman was a definite disadvantage. She wanted to be out there with him, keeping an eye on him. If anything happened to him...

Nothing was going to happen, she assured herself, doing her best to believe it. The rustlers would be fools to try again. Come the morning, the fence would be repaired and that would be that.

Sleep didn't come easily, all the same. She lay for what seemed like hours, straining her ears for any untoward sounds. Gunfire would carry for miles at night. When she did eventually doze off, it was to drift into a nightmare from which she awoke shaking in terror, though with only the vaguest memory of what the dream had been about.

Seated on the edge of the bed, Cal put out a gentle hand and smoothed the damp hair back from her forehead. 'I'm here,' he said softly.

Pure instinct brought her bolting upright into his arms, mind blanked of everything but the relief of having him there, lips seeking his with an urgency that elicited like response. He was still fully dressed, but not for long, shedding his clothes as he kissed her—tossing her nightdress after them. There were no preliminaries; he took her the way she wanted to be taken: fiercely, passionately, wordlessly, his body a driving force claiming her for his own.

It was a long time before either of them moved again afterwards. Alex was content just to lie there supporting his weight, their bodies still joined, their limbs entwined. She didn't want to think, only to feel—to remember the ravishing possession. She belonged to him with every last living part of her, now.

Cal was the first to stir, his expression difficult to decipher in the early-morning light as he lifted his head to look down at her.

'If that's how you say good morning, I can't wait for the goodnight,' he said softly. 'You're one hell of a woman, Alex Sherwood!'

'It must be the company I keep,' she parried. 'I think I was having a nightmare.'

'I know. I heard you.'

'*Heard* me?'

'You called out.' He rolled onto his back, drawing her

with him and holding her close, his hand caressing her hair. 'You said my name.'

'I was probably dreaming you were under attack by the rustlers,' she quipped, loving the feel of him against her. 'I gather they didn't turn up?'

'No.' He drew her closer still, seeking the pulse at her temple with his lips, the kiss feather-light on her skin. 'I'll leave a couple of the boys on night patrol as a precaution, but it's probable they've been scared off.'

Her voice sounded husky, her attention centred on the slow movement of his lips along her hairline. 'So you won't be going out again yourself?'

'Only if I'm called.' He reached her ear, rimming it with the very tip of his tongue, hand sliding down the length of her back to the firm curve of her bottom. 'I can think of better things to do with my nights.'

'Such as what?' she whispered, and sensed his smile.

'Such as this,' he said, and turned her under him again, lifting himself on his elbows to watch her face as he laid claim once more, eyes dark with renewed passion. 'Far, far better things!'

It was almost fully light when he finally left her. Alex lay watching him through half-closed lids as he stood up to seek his clothes, dwelling on the play of muscle across the breadth of his shoulders, the narrowness of his waist and hips, the firmness of thigh. Aroused or dormant, he was all man. The temptation to reach out and touch him—to see him come alive yet again—was almost irresistible. That he could, she didn't doubt.

Enough was enough, she told herself severely. Did she want him to think her a total wanton? She could wait till tonight—just.

Jeans zipped up, shirt hanging free and unfastened, Cal paused to look down at her, mouth curving when she failed to make any move. 'You're not asleep,' he said softly. 'I could feel you watching me.'

He sat down on the mattress edge, drawing down the sheet covering her breasts to bend and put his lips to one instantly peaking nipple. 'I could spend the rest of the day in bed with you,' he said against her skin, 'and still not have nearly enough of you. Which is why I'd better go now, while I still can,' he added with a groan, sitting upright and covering her up again.

Don't, she wanted to say as he got to his feet, but she bit it back. It was getting late. Margot and Greg would be up and around any minute now.

'You've only had a couple of hours' sleep in the last forty-eight,' she said instead. 'If Greg is going to take responsibility for the guests at all, why not leave him to it and get some rest?'

'I could do with it, I suppose,' he admitted. 'As I said before, you're an exhausting lady.' He studied her a moment longer, appraising the spread of blonde hair across the pillow, the pure lines of her face. His eyes reflected the light from the window, hiding whatever expression lurked there. 'Later,' was all he said.

The deprivation when he'd gone was acute. Wonderful as his lovemaking had been, there was little indication of any deeper involvement, thought Alex ruefully. She'd given him too much too soon; that was probably her biggest mistake. There was a lot to be said for old-fashioned morality—frustrating though it must have been to keep a man at arm's length when every fibre was crying out for fulfilment.

It was a bit late to start practising denial now, anyway, she decided. Cal would probably see it as one of those games he had accused her of playing. In any case, she

doubted her ability to say no to him. She didn't *want* to
say no to him. That way she would have nothing.

The first contingent of guests came in around eleven.
More of a mixed bag this week, Alex had already de-
duced from the guest list: a couple of singles and a family party sharing one of the larger cabins.

She hadn't seen Cal at all since he left her, although
Margot had spotted him going into the office earlier. He
came through to the dining room when they all went in
for lunch, manner cordial as always as he greeted the
newcomers.

The coolness in his eyes when their glances happened
to clash threw Alex completely. That his attitude towards
her had undergone a radical alteration was apparent,
though she couldn't for the life of her think what might
have caused the change. If they'd been on their own she
would have asked him what was wrong, but he didn't
even take a seat beside her.

She sat through the meal with her mind going round
in circles. Difficult as it was to accept after all he had
said that morning, the only explanation she could come
up with was that, having satiated his appetite, he no
longer saw any reason to keep up the pretence. Probably
one of the easiest conquests he'd ever made, she thought
numbly. Almost certainly the quickest. She hadn't even
been here a week yet.

He made no effort to approach her after the meal. He
was going into town and then over to the Circle X, she
heard him tell Greg. He could be contacted there if necessary.

Watching him drive away, Alex felt sick. He'd had
all she had to offer, now he was off to make his peace

with Diane, who would no doubt welcome him with open arms and ready forgiveness.

All in all, it was a good thing she hadn't got round to cancelling Thursday's reservation as she had planned on doing this morning, she reflected painfully. What she'd gone through back home paled into insignificance compared with the way she felt right now. She wanted to crawl into a hole and stay there.

The rest of the guests were in by three. Both men in their mid to late twenties, the two singles were totally different in type—one boyishly enthusiastic, the other weighing everything up with a shrewd eye. It was only when the latter opened his mouth that Alex recalled Cal telling her there was an Englishman booked in this week. Leo Kirby, he was called.

'I'm doing a series of articles on action holidays for *World* magazine,' he said over drinks on the veranda before supper. 'I've sampled a resort ranch, now it's the working variety's turn. From what I've seen so far, most people would go for the former. The cabins here are comfortable enough, but they're pretty basic compared with the Mountain Sky up in Montana.'

'We're not aiming for a five-star rating,' Alex returned crisply, biting her lip at the speculative expression that sprang in his eyes.

'You're family?'

'My brother is married to the owner's sister,' she acknowledged. 'I'm only here on holiday, myself. Going home Thursday,' she added with purpose, as if to confirm it in her own mind.

'So soon? Pity.' He studied her thoughtfully. 'You know, I've a feeling I've seen you somewhere before.'

'It's said we all have a *doppelgänger*,' she rejoined,

with a lightness she was far from feeling. 'Blue-eyed blondes are ten-a-penny!'

'Not all with your looks.' He was far from put off the scent. 'What do you do when you're home?'

'Secretary,' she lied, failing to take account of the probability that Margot, if no one else, would mention what she really did for a living at some point during the coming week. 'Just an ordinary secretary.'

Leo laughed. 'I'll bet your boss doesn't see you as ordinary!'

'I work for a woman,' she improvised, getting ever deeper. 'Would you like that freshening?' she asked, indicating his near-empty glass.

'Not right now, thanks. Talking of bosses,' he tagged on, 'when do we get to meet the owner himself?'

'As soon as he gets back, I—' Alex broke off at the sound of an engine, ears tuned to the engine-note, heart jerking. 'He's here now, I think.'

He came up the steps some few minutes later, pausing to say hello to the company in general. Leo got to his feet to hold out a hand, unfazed by the four-inch disparity in height.

'Kirby,' he said. '*World* magazine. You agreed to let me do a write-up on the Lazy Y. I'd like a chat, soon as you have the time. Get some gen on the place.'

'Sure,' Cal responded. 'After supper, if you like.' His glance rested momentarily on Alex, sitting on the swing-sofa she had been sharing with the journalist, his expression indefinable. 'I guess you two are finding plenty to talk about.'

The other man laughed. 'We only just got started, but we're working on it. Too bad Alex is leaving so soon.'

The grey eyes gave nothing away. 'Isn't it, though? See you at supper anyway. I need to clean up.'

'Bet he can be a real authoritarian when he wants to be,' commented Leo, dropping back onto the sofa. 'The way the two of you eyed one another just now, I'd say there was little love lost,' he added speculatively. 'Personality clash?'

'All the way.' Alex had no intention of enlarging on that statement. 'I noticed you had photographic equipment with you when you arrived. Do you always cover the whole thing yourself?'

Leo accepted the change of subject readily enough. 'Always. That way I get the whole fee. I'll be setting up some shots in the morning. You'd be doing me a favour if you'd be in one or two yourself.'

'Why?' she asked.

'Because you're extremely photogenic and it would look good. You could easily have been a model,' he tagged on, viewing her with a professional eye. 'It's a crying shame to stick that face and body away in some office! If you—'

He broke off, a new and disturbing expression crossing his face. 'Secretary be damned! I knew I'd seen you before! You were plastered all over the tabloids last month!'

It took everything Alex had to hang onto an outer composure. Denials were useless, she decided instantly; he was far too certain to be convinced by any more *doppelgänger* claims. Fortunately, no one else appeared to have overheard.

'As a journalist yourself, you should know not to take everything you read in the newspapers as fact,' she said huskily. 'I just happened to be there at the wrong time.'

She could hardly blame him too much for the scepticism she saw in his eyes; he was far from the only one to doubt her version of events. But then, who would believe anyone *could* be as naïve as she had been where someone like Morgan Baxter was concerned?

'It isn't all that important whether you believe me or not,' she said now. 'But I'd be grateful if you'd keep it to yourself.'

There was a certain calculation in Leo's regard. 'You haven't told your in-laws about it?'

'There's no reason for them to know.' Alex was doing her best not to plead.

'I guess not.' He shrugged. 'No skin off my nose.'

She heard the supper-gong ring out with relief, although she had never felt less like eating. 'Thanks.'

'You'll have to tell me your side of the story,' he said, getting up along with her. 'I like to keep an open mind.'

He was telling her rather than asking, but Alex hardly dared risk declining, much as she wanted to. She gave him a weak smile. 'If you like.'

Supper was even more of an ordeal than lunch had been. What little she managed to eat at all tasted like sawdust. Cal was seated opposite. She felt his eyes on her once or twice but couldn't bring herself to look at him. What was the point? She knew what she'd see.

Despite the promises, her heart was in her mouth the whole time he and Leo were talking together afterwards. Not that it would make any great difference now, she supposed, if her secret did come out. Cal had classed her a bimbo from the start.

Sitting there amidst the laughing, chatting crowd of vacationers, Alex felt the numbness suddenly give way to overriding anger at the thought of being used the way he had used her. Was she just going to let him get away with it scot-free? she asked herself. There might be little she could do, but there was certainly plenty she could say! If nothing else, it would relieve her feelings.

She gave him a few minutes after he went indoors, some time later, then followed him. He wasn't in the living room, and it was doubtful he would have gone to bed this early, she judged, which left the office as the most likely place to find him—providing he hadn't left the house altogether via the rear.

The anger still running white-hot inside her, she went in without bothering to knock, crashing the door to behind her as Cal looked up from the sheaf of papers he was studying. It was the first time Alex had been in the office, but she took little note of the surroundings, her attention centred on the lean, hard features.

'Already finished notching your gun, have you?' she flung at him. 'Or wouldn't the barrel take any more?' She gave him no time to reply. 'If Diane had any sense she'd tell you where to go, but I'm sure you managed to convince her I was just another passing fancy!'

Brows drawn together, Cal straightened slowly from the desk-edge where he had been leaning, eyes riveted to her antagonistic face. 'What the hell are you talking about?'

'You know darn well what I'm talking about!' she said in disgust. 'I'm a long way from being the first, and I very much doubt if I'll be the last. You're an out-and-out chauvinist, Cal. You think it fine and natural for a man to have sex where it's available, but any woman who makes it available is a trollop!'

'That depends on the woman.' He was angry himself, eyes glittering dangerously, body tensed. 'When it comes to the kind of games you like playing, the description isn't that far out.'

'If there were any games being played, you were the one doing it,' she said between her teeth. 'All that sweet talk this morning, then you look at me as if I'd just crawled out from under a stone the next time we meet!'

'What would you expect,' he demanded, 'when I'd just found out you were planning on taking off without telling anybody in a couple of days?'

CHAPTER TEN

IT WAS several seconds before Alex found her voice, mind grappling with the implications.

'How did you hear about that?' she asked, confused.

Cal regarded her with cynicism. 'The agency rang through to say they'd been unable to get you an earlier departure, and to ask for confirmation that you still wanted Thursday's reservation.'

'I made that on Saturday,' she said on a muted note. 'After what happened Friday night, I thought it best to leave as soon as possible.' She hesitated. 'What did you tell them?'

'That you'd be travelling as planned.' The grey eyes were narrowed, penetrating. 'If you'd intended cancelling at all, you'd have had plenty of time to do it before I got down this morning.'

'I did intend to,' she said. 'I just didn't get round to it.' Her smile wavery. 'Too much else to think about.' She hesitated, searching his face, still not sure of her ground. 'Was that the only reason you...turned against me?'

'It seemed a pretty good one at the time. I went to the Circle X to see Joss, not Diane, as it happens. I've no interest in her.'

Alex drew in a long, slow breath. 'I shouldn't have brought her name into it.'

'No,' he agreed. 'She isn't the issue.' He paused, the hard lines of his face relaxing a little as he studied her. 'So do I take it you're staying?'

She held his gaze, heart beating a rapid tattoo against the wall of her chest. 'If you want me to.'

'If I want you to,' he repeated softly. 'What I want—'

He broke off with a sudden, impatient gesture, crossing the space between them in a couple of strides to pull her into his arms. Alex met his mouth eagerly, passionately, hiding nothing of what she felt, of what *she* wanted.

'I love you,' she murmured thickly against his lips. 'I love you, Cal! You must know that!'

He lifted her easily and carried her across to the leather couch set against a side-wall, sitting down with her across his lap to run possessive fingers through the cascade of blonde hair spilling over his supporting arm, eyes more revealing than she had ever seen them as they perused every detail of her face.

'You'd better mean it,' he said roughly.

'I do,' she assured him. 'I never meant anything more!' She brought up her hand to trace the line of his mouth, loving the strength of it. 'I was hooked the moment I laid eyes on you.'

His lips curved. 'I guess I could say the same.'

'Shower-cap, red eyes and all?' she teased.

'Particularly the "all"—the reason I gave you a hard time at first. Greg was enough of a problem, without falling for his sister.' He shook his head as she opened her mouth, guessing what she was about to say. 'We're not discussing Greg and Margot. Right now, I'm only interested in where *we* go from here.'

He had taken his hand from her hair to cover her breast. She took the hand and kissed the horseman's hardened skin at the base of his fingers before putting it back where it belonged, looking into his eyes without concealment. 'Where do you want to go?'

'I want to set my seal on you,' he stated firmly. 'That means marriage in my book. I'm not willing to settle for anything less.'

'We've only known each other a few days,' she whispered.

'So what difference does that make?' His voice roughened. 'Unless you can't contemplate making your home here.'

She shook her head in swift denial. 'There's no place I'd rather be!'

'Then why the hesitation?'

Tell him now, urged an inner voice. Supposing Leo Kirby dropped it out? But then, why should he? she asked herself. What would he stand to gain?

'Just that I want you to be sure,' she said, pushing the whole thing to the back of her mind. 'I couldn't bear it if you decided you'd made a mistake.'

The smile came again, turning the grey to burnished silver. 'I'm not above making mistakes, but the way I feel about you isn't one of them.'

He dropped his head to find her mouth again, cherishing her lips with a tenderness that stirred her to the depths. Alex kissed him back blindly, all doubts forgotten—loving him, wanting him, needing him.

They made love on the thick, soft rug spread in front of the couch, the door locked against intruders, the world shrunk to the space within these four walls. Alex could have stayed there for ever, just the two of them. She said as much, hearing his low laugh.

'I don't somehow think we'd be left long on our own, but I appreciate the sentiment.' He watched the play of expression across her face as he moved, mouth sensual. 'You're mine now' he said thickly. 'And don't you ever forget it!'

There might have been a time when she would have taken exception to that caveat, but not now. There was no danger of her forgetting it because no other man could ever make her feel this depth of emotion, she thought passionately as her senses fused. No other man in the whole wide world!

It was gone ten when they finally emerged from the office. A faint murmur of voices drifted in from the veranda, along with the clinking of crockery. There was usually coffee on the go around this time, for anyone still up and around, or hot chocolate for those who preferred to avoid caffeine before retiring.

'We'd better go join them for the last half-hour,' said Cal. 'I could do with a stimulant!'

'If we go out together, it's going to cause a whole lot of speculation as to where we've been for the last hour or more,' Alex pointed out.

He lifted a quizzical eyebrow. 'Is it important?'

She hesitated, then said slowly, 'I'd as soon we kept it all private for a while.'

'You don't even want Greg and Margot to know?'

'Not just yet.' She made a small, appealing gesture, sensing a lack of accord. 'It's all happened so fast I can hardly believe it myself. They're going to be absolutely stunned.'

'Margot will be absolutely delighted,' Cal contended. 'She's told me more than once that you're everything a man could possibly want in a woman. She isn't far wrong either,' he added softly.

Alex assumed an indignant expression. 'Not *far* wrong!'

'Well, you need bringing into line from time to time, but I don't see it as a big problem.' Laughing, he caught the hand she pretended to aim at his cheek, swinging it behind her back to pull her to him. 'As I was saying.'

'Brute!' she accused. 'Just because you're bigger than me!'

'The one advantage I've got.' He kissed her soundly, then let her go, turning her towards the outer doors. 'You go first, if you must. I'll follow in a few minutes.'

There were only half a dozen or so people left on the veranda, Margot and Greg among them. The latter eyed her with lifted brows as she took a seat.

'Thought you'd gone to bed,' he remarked. 'There's coffee left in the pot, if you want some. Chocolate too, I think.' He watched her pour a cup, tagging on casually, 'Seen anything of Cal?'

'I think he's in the office,' Alex responded, on what she hoped was an equally casual note. She directed a smile at the rest of the group. 'Relaxing out here, isn't it? A nice end to the day.'

'Cool, though,' observed Leo Kirby. 'Your blood must run a lot thicker than mine!'

Like the others, he was wearing a sweater, while Alex had only her cotton shirt. 'I'm not going to be out long enough to feel it,' she said lightly. 'Anyway, the chocolate's hot enough.'

'Hope the coffee is too,' said Cal, joining them. He filled a cup, but didn't bother taking a seat, leaning against the rail. 'You realise you're all welcome to use the living room?' he remarked.

'I already told them that,' claimed Greg. 'Nobody wanted to be inside.'

'I spend enough time inside back home,' put in one of the other men. 'I aim to get as much fresh air as possible into my lungs this week.'

'*I* want to learn how to throw a lasso,' said his wife.

'It would come in mighty useful when I catch you sneaking off to play golf after I ask you to do some job round the house!'

Cal grinned. 'We aim to please everyone.'

The 'we' included her now, thought Alex. She stole a glance at him, thrilling as always to the masculine outline. She was going to marry this man, going to bear his children. Two of them, she mused dreamily: first a boy, then a girl. For all she knew, she was carrying already; she hadn't given the matter another thought since yesterday. Not that it really mattered any more. Cal wanted children; he had said so. So did she—providing they were his.

Thin blood or not, Leo Kirby was the last to retire to his cabin. Alex didn't much care for the conspiratorial look he gave her when he said goodnight, but no one else seemed to notice anything. If he kept his mouth shut—and there was absolutely no reason why he shouldn't—there was no need for Cal to know any of it. Why run the risk?

'One day down, five to go,' commented Greg when the journalist had departed. He looked across at his brother-in-law. 'How am I doing?'

'I'll tell you at the end of the week,' Cal returned drily. 'A lot of things could go wrong yet.' He seemed about to add something else, then apparently changed his mind, coming away from the rail to put his cup back on the tray. 'I'm for bed.'

'Me too,' said his sister, smothering a yawn. 'Greg?'

'I'll be up in a minute,' he said.

Alex sat tight, too self-conscious to go upstairs at the same time as Cal. Later, after the other two were safely out of the way, he could come to her if he wanted to.

She hoped he would want to. It would be wonderful to spend the whole night together.

'Something happened between you and Cal tonight, didn't it?' said Greg, as soon as they were on their own. 'You came out here looking as though someone had lit a lamp inside you!'

Faced with a direct question, she found it impossible to prevaricate. 'It's usual to look like that when you're in love,' she said softly. 'You must have seen it often enough in Margot.'

'It isn't Margot and me we're talking about,' he rejoined. 'How does Cal feel?'

'He wants me to marry him.' Alex had to smile at the expression on her brother's face. 'I'm still reeling myself!'

Greg made a quick recovery, regarding her with a new respect. 'And you called *me* a fast worker!'

'It wasn't like that,' she denied. 'I didn't set out with the idea of nailing him. It just...happened.'

'Sure it did.' He shook his head admiringly. 'I expected him to be interested—any man would be—but this beats all! You'll have Diane Lattimer frothing at the mouth. She's been after him for years! Not the only one either. The best catch in the area, my brother-in-law.'

'Cut it out, Greg!' Alex was regretting telling him anything. 'I wouldn't care if he didn't have two pennies to rub together!'

'You'd never have met him if he hadn't,' he pointed out. 'You're here because I'm here, and I wouldn't have been if the prospects hadn't looked good.' He held up a staying hand as she started to speak, registering the censure in her eyes. '*All* the prospects. I couldn't have done it if I hadn't felt anything at all for Margot.'

Alex subsided a little. 'But you still don't love her?'

'I'm not sure what love's supposed to feel like,' he confessed, after a moment. 'If you've cracked it, maybe you could tell me?'

'There's more to it than sex,' she said. 'A whole lot more! It's wanting to be with one person more than anyone else in the world. It's—' She broke off, shaking her head. 'It's hard to put into words that really mean anything. You'd know it if you felt it; that's the best I can do.'

Greg smiled faintly and shrugged. 'I guess I'll just have to carry on waiting for the light to dawn. In the meantime, what's the plan?'

'Plan?'

'Well, assuming you accepted the proposal, you can hardly just stay on here as of now, can you? There's the flat, for one thing.'

'I hadn't thought that far ahead,' Alex admitted. 'I doubt if Cal has, either.' She shook off the sudden sense of despondency at the idea of leaving for any reason at all. 'There's no great rush. I need time to get used to things.' She slanted a glance at her brother as another notion struck her. 'You realise that if I do marry Cal, and we have children, the ranch will go to them rather than Margot?'

The blue eyes took on a derisive glint. 'Now that's what I'd call *really* looking ahead! Believe it or believe it not, I've no ambition to be the big white chief. Thanks to you, I'm doing what I anticipated doing to start with. I'll be quite happy to continue doing it.'

'Sorry,' she said ruefully. 'I only hope Margot will see it the same way.'

'She's always known Cal would marry some day. She'll be relieved that he finished up with you and not Diane.' Greg stretched and got to his feet, looking down at her for a moment with brotherly fondness. 'We've missed out on a whole lot these last years, Alex. It's going to be great having you around!'

'If only to keep Cal off your back,' she laughed.

'That too,' he agreed with a grin. 'Although I guess he's not so bad after all.'

Quite an accolade compared with the sentiments he'd expressed a few days ago, Alex reflected as he went inside. She sat where she was for a few minutes more, savouring the crisp, cool air, the quietness broken only by an occasional snort from the direction of the corrals. It didn't seem possible that it was only five days since her arrival. She felt as if she had known this place all her life.

And Cal. She had waited years for someone like him to come along. her dream man, Tough on the outside but with a tender core she was just beginning to discover. Much as she might deplore Greg's reasons for marrying Margot, she had to agree that without him she would never have known Cal. There might be some truth in the saying that what one never had one never missed, but...

Her heart jumped into her throat as a screech-owl gave forth from a nearby tree. About time she retired for the night before she died of shock, she thought whimsically, recovering her wits as her pulses slowed down again. At least owls weren't unlucky.

Cal's door was closed, as usual. For a brief moment she contemplated going to him, but she didn't have that much confidence as yet. Unnecessary anyway, because when she opened her own door he was already there in the bed, hands clasped behind his head, chest bare and bronzed in the lamplight.

'You've been a hell of a long time,' he growled.

Alex closed the door and leaned against it, treasuring the hunger in his voice. 'I was talking to Greg. He'd guessed there was something going on, so I felt I had to tell him.'

'I wasn't the one wanting it kept secret to start with,' Cal pointed out. 'I don't give a damn *who* knows!' He held out a hand in invitation. 'Come to bed.'

She went willingly, sinking into the strong circle of his arms. There were things to be discussed, but not here and now. There were other priorities far more pressing.

Margot lost no time in expressing her delight, flying across the landing to seize Alex in a bear-hug the moment she emerged from her room the next morning.

'I knew the two of you belonged together!' she declared jubilantly. 'I just knew it! It's going to be wonderful having you here all the time! When's the wedding going to be?'

Alex held up a protesting hand, laughing at her sister-in-law's enthusiasm. 'We haven't even thought about it yet.'

'I'll bet you've not *thought* about anything very much,' said the younger girl with a sly little smile. 'I'd have come over as soon as Greg told me last night but I didn't think you'd either of you be too pleased to see me right then.' The smile widened. 'You're blushing!'

'You're enough to make anyone blush,' claimed Alex ruefully.

The hazel eyes were dancing. 'I'll bet Cal wouldn't.'

Alex doubted it too. She had no idea what time he had left her; he simply hadn't been there when she awoke this morning. He would be out and about by now, and not necessarily in for breakfast; the ranch still had to be run. Once they were married, she was going to insist on taking an active part in day-to-day affairs, she decided. No sitting at home for her!

The guests were in fine shape after a good night's sleep, eager to get started on the programmed events.

Leo Kirby was the only one not going on the morning ride. Lounging on the veranda in the morning sun, a notebook opened on his knee, he viewed her meditatively as she turned from the rail.

'You don't ride?' he asked.

'Not just now,' she said. 'Maybe later.'

He slanted a smile. 'Waiting for the boss to take you?'

She was reading double meanings where they didn't exist, Alex told herself. She summoned a smile of her own. 'I'm quite capable of going out alone. I just don't feel like it at present. I'd have thought you'd want to sample everything first-hand yourself, though?'

'I'm not a particular horse-lover,' he said. 'It's what's on offer as a whole I'm here to judge. I'll be taking a trip into town, this morning, to get some local colour. Maybe you'd like to come with me? I could do with the company. Particularly *your* company,' he added with soft emphasis.

Alex had seen that look in a man's eyes too often to make the mistake of doubting her instincts this time. The only way to deal with it was to leave no doubt in his mind of her total uninterest.

'Thanks, but no thanks,' she said steadily. 'Lunch is twelve-thirty, in case you didn't get round to reading your brochure yet. You should make it back in time.'

'Can you afford to be uppity, in your position?' he remarked as she started towards the door.

Arrested in mid-stride, Alex turned slowly back to look at him, registering the sardonic gleam. Her voice, when she found it, sounded rough. 'What are you saying, exactly?'

He shrugged briefly. 'Self-evident, I'd have thought. You scratch my back and I'll scratch yours.'

She drew a deep breath, doing her best to keep her nerve. 'You mean be nice to you, or you'll pass on what you think you know about me?'

'Not just what *I* think, sweetheart. I can have press-cuttings faxed through in no time.'

'Cal doesn't have a fax,' she said numbly, not at all certain that he didn't.'

'I dare say there's a newspaper office in town who'll let me use theirs.' Leo wasn't giving an inch. 'Maybe you're sure enough of him to run the risk. On the other hand, maybe not.'

Alex could feel her legs trembling but she refused to take a seat. 'What makes you think he'd have any interest either way? You said yourself there was obviously no love lost between us.'

'That was before supper. It was more than obvious that you'd straightened things out later.' Leo shook his head. 'Stop wriggling. I've got you in a cleft stick and we both know it! Either you come through for me or you take the chance. Personally, I wouldn't. Forrester doesn't come across as the type to forgive and forget too easy.'

He studied her for a moment, expression unrelenting. 'You've twenty-four hours to think about it. Never let it be said that I drive too hard a bargain!'

Alex forced herself into movement, hardly knowing where she was going, hardly caring where she was going, providing it was far enough away from that scum back there! She had met some unsavoury types over the years, but he beat all—Morgan Baxter included.

Blackmail was what it amounted to. Punishable by law, if she only had the guts to take that course.

Only she didn't; she knew that already. Any more than she had the courage to tell Cal what was going on. The fact that she had lied about her reasons for giving up modelling was damning enough in itself. How could he trust her to be telling the truth about anything?

CHAPTER ELEVEN

CAL and the boys rode in just after twelve. Watching them from the bedroom window as they unsaddled their horses, Alex was reminded of that first evening. Had anyone told her then that within a week she would be in love with the boss of the Lazy Y and he with her, she would have told them that things like that didn't happen in real life.

Only they did, didn't they? Not just the good things, but the bad ones too. That Leo Kirby would carry out his threat if she didn't comply with his demands she was in no doubt. His kind would use any method available to get what they wanted, no matter how dirty.

So far as she could see, she had three choices. She could tell Cal the truth herself, she could give Leo what he was after, or she could stall the rat for a further twenty-four hours and take the flight she hadn't yet got round to cancelling.

The second was definitely out, which brought it down to two: face the music or run away. *That* was the decision she had to make.

Lunch was an ordeal. With Leo seated opposite she couldn't avoid meeting his eyes from time to time, try as she might. He would probably be courting trouble for himself too if he did as he had threatened; whatever Cal believed, he would hardly condone the tactics. Seeing the man thrown out on his ear wouldn't be much solace, though, when she was likely to be following.

'Alex?' Cal's voice jerked her out of her thoughts to

167

face his quizzical gaze. 'Mrs. Hailwood asked you whether you might be on any of the London Underground billboards.'

'Margot was telling us about your modelling career,' said the woman in question. 'We were in London a few weeks ago. I'm pretty sure I saw you in one of those hair product ads.'

From somewhere Alex found the ability to shrug her shoulders, to say lightly, 'It's possible. I did a shampoo ad not so long ago.'

'I'm not surprised.' The woman cast an admiring glance at the gleaming gold tresses. 'I'd kill for hair like yours!'

'Wouldn't do you much good in the electric chair,' put in her husband, drawing a general laugh.

'The Underground's not the only place you might have spotted her,' said Leo, on a casual note not meant to deceive. 'You've done some top-class cover work too, haven't you?'

Alex forced herself to look at him directly, though she couldn't quite control the jerkiness in her voice. 'You must be getting me mixed up with someone else. I was never in that bracket.'

Another voice chimed in from the other end of the table with some comment on that morning's ride, drawing attention away, to Alex's relief. Leo gave her a meaningful smile, leaving her in no doubt of his continuing campaign.

'My mistake.'

It was a mistake on her part to glance in Cal's direction at that precise moment. The dark brows were drawn together, his gaze penetrating. That he had recognised some untoward element in the exchange was more than obvious, though he said nothing. He wouldn't be content to leave it there, of course. He would want to know what was going on. The question was, could she bring herself to tell him?

Leo went to his cabin after lunch, while Greg and Margot gathered their flock for a session of rope-throwing, with one of the older hands to show how it was done.

'You don't have to go out again?' Alex asked Cal, half hoping he would say he did.

'I don't *have* to do anything,' he returned drily. 'Boss's privilege. Let's get saddled up. Something I want to show you.'

They took Minty and Jingo. Jed, Cal said, deserved a rest after a morning's work. The gelding behaved himself perfectly under the firm male hand. It was Minty who played up a little this time, perhaps sensing her rider's lack of concentration.

Cal made no comment, but his expression wasn't encouraging. Whatever he was thinking might be bothering her, it couldn't come close to the reality, Alex reflected hollowly. If she had opened up that first night, when he'd suggested that she might be running away from something, there could have been a chance of his believing her version of events—but the fact that she was doing it only under duress had to go against her. A quick, clean break had to be better in the long run than seeing the disillusionment dawn. *Anything* was better than that!

She hadn't been taking a great deal of notice of where they were heading. Rounding a jutting shoulder of the mountain, she saw another, smaller valley stretched before her. A jewel of a place, green and verdant, within easy reach of the homestead yet totally out of sight of it. An elbow of river curved in and out along the perimeter.

'Hidden Creek,' said Cal. 'How would you feel about building a house here?'

'You already have a house,' she said heavily.

'But little privacy. Greg and Margot need to be on hand to deal with the guests, but we don't. I always had a fancy for this spot.'

Alex could see why. She could even imagine the kind of house: timber-built to blend with the landscape. What she couldn't see was a future with the two of them together in it.

'You don't look very enthused,' Cal observed, viewing her constrained expression. 'You'd rather share a home?'

'No, of course not,' she said. 'It's just that...' She paused, searching her mind for some plausible excuse. 'Everything has happened so fast I can't think straight,' she finished lamely. 'This time yesterday we weren't even talking to one another!'

'That was yesterday.' Cal hadn't shifted his gaze from her face. 'Is there something you're not telling me?'

Her whole body tautened like a bow-string, heart jerking. If ever there was a moment to unload this was it, but she couldn't form the words.

'Such as what?' she prevaricated.

'Such as how you and Kirby have met before, maybe?'

'Of course we haven't!' That much, at least, she could say with truth. 'What on earth makes you think we might have?'

'The two of you looked pretty familiar together when I got in last night.'

'We're both English; we'd naturally gravitate together.'

'That's what I told myself—until this lunchtime. What was all that about cover work?'

'A mistake, like he said.' Alex abandoned whatever inclination towards disclosure still lingered, taking refuge in anger. 'Am I going to be put through this catechism over every man I happen to exchange a few words with?'

Minty shifted nervously, sensing the electricity in the atmosphere. In the moment or two it took to calm the mare, Alex got a grip on herself. If leaving was the only option she could countenance, then she had to make it clear to him now.

'I think I got rather carried away last night,' she said gruffly. 'Too fast and too far. I...can't marry you, Cal. I'm sorry.'

The grey eyes were steely, jaw set rock-hard. 'Just like that?'

'No, not *just* like that! I've thought about nothing else all morning.' She kept her head bent, eyes on the hand she was using to stroke Minty's neck, too afraid of what he might see in them if she looked at him directly. 'Nobody falls in love in a few days. Not real love. All we've got is physical attraction, and that isn't enough to build a marriage on.'

'No,' he said shortly, 'I can see it wouldn't be.' He paused, tone dispassionate when he spoke again. 'So what do you have in mind?'

There was a hard obstruction in her throat, making speech difficult. 'I'm going to take that flight on Thursday.'

'What about Greg?'

'He doesn't need me.'

'True. You already served your purpose.'

Her head jerked up. 'My purpose?'

'To soften me up on his behalf.'

'It wasn't like that!' Alex could avoid his gaze no longer, flinching at the cynicism she saw there. 'He never asked for help in any direction.'

'Sure he didn't!'

'It's true.' She swallowed, struggling to stay on top of her emotions. 'You won't take the job away from him again, will you?'

The shrug was brief. 'That's a decision you won't be involved in.' Knuckles white where they gripped the rein, he brought Jingo's head round. 'Let's get back.'

It hadn't been a comfortable journey out, but it was far worse returning. Alex had never felt so utterly desolate. There was still time to change her mind and go for broke, only she knew she wouldn't. It was bad this way, but still better than the other.

The lasso lessons were still in progress, amidst much laughter and ribald comment. Margot was talking animatedly with the other man who was here on his own. Getting along like a house on fire, Alex judged, going across to join the group after taking her saddle to the barn.

'So who's doing good so far?' she asked with assumed cheerfulness.

'They all are,' claimed the wrangler doing the teaching, tongue tucked firmly into cheek. 'Have 'em bulldogging before the week's out!'

Margot waved her over. 'You didn't get to meet Dane, yet, did you?' she said. 'He's from New York!' The way she said it made it sound like the other side of the world.

Alex smiled and nodded at the young man, liking his pleasant features and unassuming manner. 'Long way to come.'

'Not as far as you,' he said. 'Congratulations, by the way.'

Alex felt her face stiffen. 'Thanks,' she got out.

'You haven't had a row already!' exclaimed Margot, obviously recognising some lack of enthusiasm. She looked across to where Cal was talking with a couple of the other hands by the adjoining corral, pulling a face. 'I'll bet it's his fault!'

'Mine, actually.' It was as much as Alex felt able to say for the moment. 'I think I'll go and find a long, cool drink,' she added. 'See you later.'

There was no sign of Leo up at the house, to her relief. All the same, she didn't linger on the veranda. Cal was right, she supposed. The only real privacy to be found was in the bedroom. Neither Margot nor Greg seemed bothered by the lack of it, but she could imagine it might have become irksome to her after a while.

Of no consequence now, though, was it? she thought bitterly.

She whiled away the rest of the afternoon packing. There was tomorrow to get through yet, but no reason to wait until the last minute. No matter how much she might wish it, nothing was going to change. Men like Leo Kirby didn't suddenly acquire consciences.

Dane wasn't the only one Margot had imparted the news to, it appeared. The best wishes rained down thick and fast at supper. Cal made no attempt to put things straight and Alex didn't have the heart to upset Margot's apple cart in front of everyone, although both she and Greg would have to be told at some point soon, of course.

Leo offered his felicitations with a look that made her long for the courage to tell him to go to hell, especially on seeing the hard irony in Cal's eyes when she caught his glance. Nothing to the look that would be there if he ever saw those press cuttings, she thought, but it was little comfort.

He disappeared after supper, to where she had no idea. Cornering her some time later, Greg lost little time in coming to the point.

'You two are acting pretty odd for a couple planning to get hitched,' he commented with brotherly candour. 'Margot thinks you've just had some kind of disagreement—*I* think it's a bit more than that. Who's right?'

They had to know some time, Alex reminded herself, biting back the instinctive denial. Tonight or tomorrow. What difference did it make?

'We're not,' she said, low-toned. 'Getting married, I mean. We…made a mistake.'

'Mutual agreement?' he queried after a moment.

'Yes.' It was one more lie, but she was past caring. Cal would be unlikely to contradict the assertion anyway. 'We both realised we didn't have enough going for us.' She gave a wry shrug. 'Better now than later. It's just rather embarrassing having everybody thinking we're a couple.'

'Margot wasn't to know this was going to happen,' Greg defended. 'Nobody told her to keep it to herself.'

'I know. I'm not blaming her. I'm the one who should have kept a closed mouth.' Alex studied the handsome features, momentarily distracted. 'Nice to hear you sticking up for her.'

'I'd always stick up for her.' He glanced across to where his wife was sitting, Dane at her side, his face darkening as the two of them burst out laughing at some shared joke. 'And I'll be sticking one on *him*, if he doesn't watch it!' he growled. 'He's been after her since he got here!'

'Perhaps he just finds her good to be with,' Alex suggested mildly. 'A sympathetic ear and all that. He doesn't come across as a woman-chaser.'

'The quiet ones are often the worst.' Greg was not to be mollified. 'We had a guy here last month you'd have sworn was only just out of the egg, until he got caught with somebody else's partner in the barn.'

'It takes two,' Alex pointed out. 'Margot wouldn't look at another man that way. Not unless she gets fed-up with loving one who doesn't love her back,' she tagged on deliberately.

An unwilling smile tugged at her brother's mouth. 'Maybe I'm closer to it than I thought. I certainly wouldn't want to lose her.' He gave the pair of them a final scrutiny then turned resolutely away. 'Anyway, that's another matter. What do you plan on doing now?'

'Simple,' she said, returning reluctantly to her own problems. 'I'm going home.'

'Another mutual decision?'

Alex lifted her shoulders again. 'There isn't much point in my staying any longer.'

'I don't see why not. If you gave it a bit more time...'

'It wouldn't alter anything.' Her tone was flat. 'I already have a flight booked on Thursday.'

'*That* soon!' Greg both looked and sounded dismayed. 'What am I going to tell Margot?'

'The same thing I've told you, I expect.' Alex was fast coming to the end of her tether. 'I think I'll have a stroll down to the corrals, and then an early night,' she said, stirring herself. 'I really don't feel like making idle conversation.'

They were seated close enough to the step for no one else to notice as she slipped away—or so she hoped. Right now, all she wanted was to be on her own. It might be better if she left tomorrow instead of waiting till Thursday morning, she thought hollowly. She could always spend the night in Sheridan.

There were a dozen or so horses in each of the corrals, but neither Minty, Jed nor Jingo were among them. Standing on a lower rail, with her chin propped on the bent arms she rested along the top, Alex spoke softly to a couple of the nearer animals, seeing ears prick and heads turn in recognition. She was going to miss this almost as much as she would miss Cal, she acknowledged, fighting tears. Everything she could ever want was here.

So take a chance, urged a voice at the back of her mind. Tell him the whole story. If he feels anything at all for you, he'll believe you!

'Still thinking about it?' asked another voice behind her on an unpleasant note. 'You don't really have a lot of choice, you know. Not if you want to keep what you've got.'

Alex let herself down slowly to the ground, taking care not to slide her hands along the wood. The last thing she needed at the moment was another splinter. It took everything she had to make herself turn and look at the man who was ruining her life without spitting in his face.

Standing there in the moonlight, hands thrust casually into the pockets of his jeans, he looked so innocuous—the antithesis of the type that might be expected to behave the way he was doing. Greg was right, she thought. One could never tell.

'You're so low, you could crawl under a worm and still have clearance!' she said contemptuously.

Leo laughed, obviously more amused at than disturbed by the invective. 'Nice turn of phrase. I must remember that one.'

He studied her insolently, letting his eyes drift down the length of her body and back again, registering the expression on her face with more amusement. 'Oh, come on! It's hardly the first time you've had a man look you over.'

'The first time by a bloodsucker!' she gritted. 'You're not fit to be called a man!'

'Sticks and stones,' he mocked. 'They won't make me change my mind, so you may as well save your breath. If you don't want Forrester to know what you've been up to, you'll start tomorrow in a better frame of mind. And just to aid the decision...'

He paused to pull a folded paper from his back pocket, tossing it to the ground at her feet when she made no attempt to take it from him. 'You might like to refresh your memory. It's not the only copy, by the way.' He lifted a hand in taunting salute. 'See you.'

Alex stayed where she was as he sauntered off. Only when he was almost back at the house did she finally stoop to pick up the paper. She knew what it was, of course; she had used fax machines herself.

The moonlight was bright enough to read by, the reproduction good and clear. Eyes lit by desire, lips parted in sensual invitation, her face occupied central position. Lifted from an advertisement for aftershave, if she remembered correctly. There was another photograph further down, taken when she had left the police station after her night in the cells, hair in need of a brush, dress looking as though she'd slept in it—which she hadn't, not having slept at all.

Morgan himself had scorned her claim that she hadn't known what he had in mind when he invited her to spend an evening with him at one of his clubs. Even when faced with the evidence it had taken her a while to realise what was going on behind the scenes, and that she had been expected to jump at the chance to become one of his highly-paid 'entertainers'.

He'd been attempting to persuade her when the police had raided the place in search of the drugs he'd been trafficking as a sideline. Finding her in the back office with him, they'd rounded her up along with the rest. She'd been released from custody the following day due to lack of evidence that she had been involved in either venture, but too late to stop the Press from getting hold of her name.

The column reproduced here was by no means the only report filed, just the most damning: a tightrope of innuendo. Several people had said she had grounds to sue, but she couldn't have faced any more publicity.

Any more than she could face Cal now with this, she acknowledged. The few people who knew her well enough might be prepared to give her the benefit of the doubt, but Cal only knew her in the physical sense. The very fact that she had proved so 'easy' with him would go against her.

Unwilling to be drawn into conversation on the veranda, she went round to the rear of the house, trusting that Buck would be long gone from the kitchen he considered his private domain. Some of the boys were taking it easy outside the bunk house, Royd not among them, she was thankful to see. He hadn't forgiven her yet for what he obviously still considered to be encouragement on her part. No doubt he wouldn't be sorry to see the back of her either.

It was still barely nine o'clock when she reached her room, but she had no intention of venturing out again. She finished her packing, all except a clean shirt for tomorrow and the trouser-suit she had travelled in. Still not a full week ago yet. It hardly seemed possible. She had lived a lifetime just today.

She finally fell into bed around eleven, though not to sleep. With a window opened, she could hear the good-nights being called as people started to drift away to their own beds. Normally there would have been a chuck-wagon barbecue out on the range tonight, but it had been rescheduled for tomorrow due to some problem with the wagon itself. Difficult to get out of without advertising the rift to all and sundry—although they'd know soon enough when she departed.

Deep down, she was still hoping for some change of heart on Leo's part, she admitted wryly. 'Grasping at straws' it was called. He wasn't going to relent. No one capable of coming up with such an odious scheme in the first place was likely to suffer an attack of conscience. She was stuck with the same two choices, one of which she had already dismissed.

Lying there, she heard Margot and Greg come up, the two of them giggling like school children. At least *that* relationship was starting to look as if it might have some staying power. There was no sound from next door. For all she knew, Cal wasn't even in the house.

It could have been mere minutes, it could have been an hour later when the door quietly opened. Jerked out of the torpid state into which she had sunk, Alex came upright as Cal closed it equally quietly behind him, pausing with his back to the wood, much as she had done herself the night before, his expression masked by the semi-darkness.

'What do you want?' she asked thickly.

'You,' he said on a harsh note. 'I think you owe me that much.'

He moved towards her, unbuttoning his shirt as he came, tugging it free of his jeans to shrug it from his shoulders and drop it to the floor, fingers seeking his belt-buckle with the same inexorable intent.

'I'm not taking no for an answer,' he declared, 'so don't bother saying it. If we've nothing else, we've this!'

Alex was silent, unable to force her voice through the hard ache in her throat. There was no thought in her mind to say no. Not with every inch of her already clamouring for his touch, her senses fired by the sight of him as he shed the last of his clothing and stood before her, magnificent in his masculine nudity. She would carry this memory with her for the rest of her life.

Whatever anger he was feeling inside, there was no hint of it when he sat down on the bed to take her face between his two hands and put his lips first to one closed eye and then the other. Coming on top of the harshness, the tenderness of it made her want to weep. Her lips were parted, trembling in anticipation when he reached them, her arms creeping about his neck to draw him closer as he kissed her, mind blanked of everything but the need to be with him again—a part of him. Beyond that she didn't want to think.

He drew her nightdress straps down over her arms, kissing each portion of newly exposed flesh as the silk slid away, running his tongue around each tingling, peaking nipple with a lightness that left her aching for more; carrying on downwards, over quivering stomach muscles and tremoring abdomen, in the wake of the garment to claim the ultimate intimacy.

Alex was lost in an emotional blizzard, lips forming words without volition, fingers digging deep into the thick dark hair. Then he was moving back up her slender length, joining his body to hers, the feeling exquisite in its possessive power. And she was moving with him, slowly at first, then faster, the darkness revolving, becoming a vortex drawing her into its bottomless depths.

Whether she fell genuinely asleep or simply drifted in limbo for a time, she couldn't be sure. It took the draught of cool air on her skin when Cal moved away from her to bring her out of it.

'Don't go,' she whispered, before she could stop herself.

'I've no intention of going,' he said. 'Not now.' He lifted himself on an elbow, looking down at her with an ardour even the darkness couldn't hide. 'I've no intention of letting you go either. Whatever reason you had for trying to make out you didn't feel enough for me, you were lying through your teeth. You feel the same way I do.'

He brought up a hand to trace a fingertip gently across her lips. 'Say it, Alex. The way you did a few minutes ago. *Say* it!'

She could no more have denied him than stop breathing, regardless of where it must inevitably lead. Her voice came out husky. 'I love you.'

He gave a long-drawn sigh, the taut lines of his face relaxing a little. 'So why the pretence?'

It was her turn to sigh. 'There's something you have to know about me. Something that might make you think again.' She hesitated, searching for a way to start, then came to a decision. 'Easier if you read it for yourself.'

Cal came to a sitting position as she slid away from him to reach into the drawer where she had put the fax. He took it from her with brows drawn together and reached behind him to switch on the bedside lamp.

Unable to bring herself to watch his face as he read, Alex concentrated her gaze on the broad, bronzed shoulders and smoothly muscled arms, remembering both the power and the gentleness contained there. The words he was reading were emblazoned on her mind, the headline alone a damning indictment.

SEX FOR SALE!
Top model arrested in raid

Police yesterday raided the Barrington Club, arresting the owner Morgan Baxter, 36, on suspicion of living off immoral earnings. It is rumoured that among club members were a number of VIPs, judges and politicians, though no names have been released by police except for that of his girlfriend, model Alex Sherwood, arrested alongside Baxter.

Miss Sherwood, an attractive blonde, 24, looked drawn and pensive as she was released after a night in the cells. She denied any involvement in the club or knowledge of Baxter's activities and stressed that her relationship with Baxter was one of platonic friendship. It is believed that Sherwood immediately left the country.

Apart from a certain tension in the line of his jaw, it was difficult to tell what Cal might be thinking when he lifted his gaze at last.

'You had this faxed through yourself?' he asked.

Alex shook her head. 'I wasn't even going to tell you about it. At least...not just yet.'

'Then who—?' He broke off, eyes acquiring a sudden icy glitter as his mind made the leap. 'Kirby! It's Kirby, isn't it?'

'Yes.' Alex could hardly get the words out. 'He recognised me from the newspaper coverage and threatened to show you that if I didn't do as he wanted.'

The glitter increased. 'And what was it he wanted?'

'Me,' she said, low-toned. 'Not permanently of course.'

'So you could have bought him off and I'd have been none the wiser.'

'I could have,' she agreed. 'If I really were the kind of person suggested there, I probably would have. On the other hand, if I weren't such a coward he wouldn't have been able to blackmail me to start with. I should have told you about it, Cal. It wasn't fair to hide something like that from you for fear—'

She broke off, heart lurching painfully as he dropped the incriminating fax and got abruptly to his feet to reach for his discarded clothing. So that was that; he wasn't prepared to listen to any more.

'Stay put,' he clipped out, fastening his belt as he moved towards the door. 'I'll be back.'

Late as it was, he was going to confront Leo, she guessed. Not that the journalist could tell him anything more damning than what he had already read. When he did come back, it would only be to give her her marching orders, she was sure.

It seemed a year, but was probably about twenty minutes, before the door opened once more. Cal came in and closed it behind him, looking across at her as she sat propped on the bed in her wrap, the lamp she had left lit not strong enough to reveal much of his expression.

Only when he moved forward to the end of the bed did Alex note the rip in his shirt-sleeve where it joined the shoulder, his general dishevelment. The knuckles of his right hand were skinned too.

'What have you done?' she breathed.

'Given him something to think about for the rest of the night,' he said with satisfaction. 'He'll be on his way first thing in the morning.'

'He's hardly going to be turning in a favourable report

on the Lazy Y after this,' was all Alex could think of to say.

'I guess not.' Cal neither looked nor sounded concerned at the prospect. He studied her for a moment, taking in the pallor of her face, the tumbled, finger-raked blonde hair and darkened blue eyes, his expression sobering. 'Want to tell me the real story?'

'You don't think that's it?' she whispered, indicating the fax sheet still lying where he had dropped it.

'If I did, I wouldn't be here.'

He moved again, with purpose, coming round to take a seat on the bed-edge and pull her into his arms. The kiss was spirit-lifting in its sheer intensity of feeling. Alex buried her face in his shoulder when it ended, too overcome to speak for a moment or two.

'How will you know whether I'm telling the truth or not when you've only known me a few days?' she asked haltingly.

'Because you don't have it in you to be what that rag is trying to make you out to be,' he said simply. 'I may have had some pre-set ideas about you before you got here, but you soon knocked them out of me. Whatever you were doing in that place when it was raided, you weren't involved with either drugs or prostitution. I'd stake my life on that.' He held her away from him so that he could see her face. 'You don't have to tell me anything if you don't want to.'

She didn't want to, because she still couldn't believe that he really did have that much faith in her. Drugs and prostitution aside, she *had* been involved with a man no woman in her right mind would have considered a thoroughly 'honest Joe'. She was no gullible teenager. When Cal got down to thinking about it, he was going to come to the rightful conclusion that she must have had *some* suspicions about the man.

'I think I have to,' she said quietly. 'You've a right to know.' She drew in a long, slow breath, searching for the words.

'I met Morgan when I was doing some promotional work for one of his companies. I suppose I was flattered when he started paying me a lot of attention. Enough to turn a deaf ear to any doubts I had about his business interests—although it certainly never occurred to me that he might be doing what he was.'

'You thought he might be into some kind of financial racket?' Cal's voice was steady, giving little away.

'Yes. No excuse, I know, but it made him no worse than many others.'

'You've been mixing with the wrong kind of people for far too long,' came the soft growl. 'How long were you seeing him before that night?'

'A couple of weeks or so. I didn't sleep with him,' she added swiftly. 'I might have been all kinds of a fool for getting mixed up with him at all, but I'd have drawn the line at that.'

This time she forced herself to meet the grey eyes, anticipating a certain scepticism at the very least—relieved beyond measure when she found none. 'Not that he brought any pressure to bear in that direction anyway. Apparently, he never touched the girls he had it in mind to hire.'

'No mixing business with pleasure?'

'So it seems. It wasn't so much a physical attraction on my part to start with. More of a...mesmerisation, I suppose you could call it.' She gave a short laugh. 'It sounds ridiculous now, but I didn't even realise what kind of place that club of his was until he took me into the office and tried persuading me to work for him.'

Her voice faltered a little at the memory, but she kept going. 'He could have put the police right about me right away, but he didn't. His way of paying me back for refusing to become one of his girls, I imagine. The only reason they let me go was because none of the other girls would back him up—only it was too late by then. The Press had got hold of it.' Her smile was brittle. 'One way to achieve overnight fame!'

'Would you have come out here to see Greg if it hadn't been for wanting to get away from it all for a spell?' Cal asked softly.

'I don't know,' she said. 'Maybe not.'

'Then I owe this Morgan character that much.'

Alex looked at him with misty emotion. 'If we'd never met, we'd never have known we were missing anything.'

'I'd have known.' It was said with certainty. 'I've waited a long time for that vital spark. It was there right away—for both of us. You knew as well as I did that we were going to be lovers at some not very far distant point.'

Her smile held a hint of her usual vitality. 'The thought never crossed my mind!'

'Liar,' he said. 'I saw your reaction when I touched you.'

The way she was reacting now at the very memory, she could have told him. The way she felt every time she saw him—or even just thought about him: aroused. He was right; she had known. From that very first moment when she had seen him unsaddling Jed, she had known. The antagonism had simply been a defence against that knowledge.

'What about what I've just told you?' she said, sobering again. 'Doesn't it make a difference?'

The hand that lifted to caress her cheek was a reassurance in itself, the look that accompanied the gesture even more so. 'Stop being so hard on yourself. You made a mistake, and paid for it. Put it down to experience and forget about it.'

'Can you?' she asked, and saw a teasing light leap in the grey eyes.

'Forget I'm marrying a jailbird? Not easy!' Grinning, he seized the fist she raised in mock threat, pushing her back down into the pillows and pinning her there. 'No violence! I'm bigger than you, remember.'

'In every way,' she said softly. She took his hand and pressed her lips to the skinned knuckles, tasting the blood he had shed on her behalf. 'I don't deserve you, Cal.'

'No, well, I'll have to let you make it up to me.' His gaze kindled as he looked down at her. 'You're all I could ever want, Alex. Everything I ever hoped to find in a woman.'

'More than Diane Lattimer had to offer?' She regretted the question the moment it was out, shaking her head in swift negation. 'Forget I said that.'

It was Cal's turn to shake his head. 'If you needed to say it then it needed to be said.' He paused, eyes holding hers. 'There was never a time when I considered marrying Diane. You're the only woman I've ever been able to contemplate spending the rest of my life with.'

Blue eyes lit with sudden humour as the last doubts vanished. 'Even though I'm likely to get out of line sometimes?'

The strong mouth widened in response. 'I dare say I

can handle it. Question is, can you handle being married to a chauvinist?'

'Until I get you retrained, sure,' she said. 'What we need round here is a little more PC.'

'PC?' Cal queried, with a quizzical lift of an eyebrow.

'Passionate kissing,' she translated, melting afresh as she looked into the lean face. 'Like this...'

A long time later, Cal murmured lazily, 'I was under the impression that kissing began with a K not a C.'

'Does it really?' she said in guileless tones. 'I never was much good at spelling.'

Coming Next Month

HARLEQUIN PRESENTS®

THE BEST HAS JUST GOTTEN BETTER!

#1929 A MARRIAGE TO REMEMBER Carole Mortimer
Three years ago Adam Carmichael had walked out on Maggi—now he was back! Divorce seemed the only way to get him out of her life for good. But Adam wasn't going to let her go without a fight!

#1930 RED-HOT AND RECKLESS Miranda Lee
(Scandals!)
Ben Sinclair just couldn't put his schoolboy obsession with Amber behind him. She *still* thought she could have anything because she was rich and beautiful. But now Ben had a chance to get even with her at last....

#1931 TIGER, TIGER Robyn Donald
Leo Dacre was determined to find out what had happened to his runaway half brother, but Tansy was just as determined not to tell him! It was a clash of equals...so who would be the winner?

#1932 FLETCHER'S BABY Anne McAllister
Sam Fletcher never ran away from difficult situations, so when Josie revealed that she was expecting his child, marriage seemed the practical solution. And he wasn't going to take no for an answer!

#1933 THE SECRET MOTHER Lee Wilkinson
(Nanny Wanted!)
Caroline had promised herself that one day she would be back for Caitlin. Now, four years later, she's applying for the job of her nanny. Matthew Carran, the interviewer, doesn't *seem* to recognize her. But he has a hidden agenda....

#1934 HUSBAND BY CONTRACT Helen Brooks
(Husbands and Wives)
For Donato Vittoria, marriage was a lifetime commitment. Or so Grace had thought—until she'd discovered his betrayal, and fled. But in Donato's eyes he was still her husband, and he wanted her back in his life—and in his bed!

As Seen on TV!

Free Gift Offer

With a Free Gift proof-of-purchase
from any Harlequin® book, you can receive
a beautiful cubic zirconia pendant.

This stunning marquise-shaped stone is a genuine cubic
zirconia—accented by an 18" gold tone necklace.
(Approximate retail value $19.95)

Send for yours today...
compliments of ✦ HARLEQUIN®

To receive your free gift, a cubic zirconia pendant, send us one original proof-of-purchase, photocopies not accepted, from the back of any Harlequin Romance®, Harlequin Presents®, Harlequin Temptation®, Harlequin Superromance®, Harlequin Intrigue®, Harlequin American Romance®, or Harlequin Historicals® title available at your favorite retail outlet, together with the Free Gift Certificate, plus a check or money order for $1.65 U.S./$2.15 CAN. (do not send cash) to cover postage and handling, payable to Harlequin Free Gift Offer. We will send you the specified gift. Allow 6 to 8 weeks for delivery. Offer good until December 31, 1997, or while quantities last. Offer valid in the U.S. and Canada only.

Free Gift Certificate

Name: _____

Address: _____

City: _____ State/Province: _____ Zip/Postal Code: _____

Mail this certificate, one proof-of-purchase and a check or money order for postage and handling to: HARLEQUIN FREE GIFT OFFER 1997. In the U.S.: 3010 Walden Avenue, P.O. Box 9071, Buffalo NY 14269-9057. In Canada: P.O. Box 604, Fort Erie, Ontario L2Z 5X3.

FREE GIFT OFFER
084-KEZ

ONE PROOF-OF-PURCHASE

To collect your fabulous FREE GIFT, a cubic zirconia pendant, you must include this original proof-of-purchase for each gift with the properly completed Free Gift Certificate.

084-KEZR